Praise for Marie Ferrarella

"Expert storytelling coupled with an engaging plot makes this an excellent read."
—*RT Book Reviews* on *Cavanaugh Undercover*

"Strong writing, good pacing, sizzling chemistry and cool tension is plentiful in this lively read."
—*RT Book Reviews* on *Mission: Cavanaugh Baby*

"A thrilling intrigue with just the right amount of sizzle to keep the pages turning faster and faster."
—*RT Book Reviews* on *Racing Against Time*

"Marie Ferrarella brings readers back for a visit with her Cavanaugh Justice family and, once again, raw emotion, hot sex and real characters rule!"
—*RT Book Reviews* on *The Strong Silent Type*

"Sizzles with sexual tension, and the plot is edgy, dark and suspenseful. Ferrarella has penned a guaranteed page-turner!"
—*RT Book Reviews* on *Internal Affair*

"*In Broad Daylight* combines danger and conspiracy with breathtaking desire to produce an electrifying read!"
—*The Romance Readers Connection*

"Ms Ferrarella creates fiery, strong-willed characters, an intense conflict and an absorbing premise no reader could possibly resist."
—*RT Book Reviews* on *A Match for Morgan*

***

Be sure to check out the next books in this exciting new series: **Cavanaugh Justice**
Where the law and passion collide

CAVANAUGH FORTUNE

BY
MARIE FERRARELLA

MILLS & BOON

Published in Great Britain 2015
by Mills & Boon, an imprint of Harlequin (UK) Limited,
Eton House, 18-24 Paradise Road, Richmond, Surrey, TW9 1SR

© 2015 Marie Rydzynski-Ferrarella

ISBN: 978-0-263-25411-2

18-0415

Harlequin (UK) Limited's policy is to use papers that are natural, renewable and recyclable products and made from wood grown in sustainable forests. The logging and manufacturing processes conform to the legal environmental regulations of the country of origin.

Printed and bound in Spain
by CPI, Barcelona

USA TODAY bestselling and RITA® Award-winning author **Marie Ferrarella** has written more than two hundred fifty books for Mills & Boon, some under the name Marie Nicole. Her romances are beloved by fans worldwide. Visit her website, www.marieferrarella.com.

To Tahra Seplowin
Welcome to Happy Chaos

Prologue

Detective Alexander Brody opened the front door of his ground-floor garden apartment, bent down and picked up the morning paper from his doorstep.

As was his habit every morning, he took the paper inside and dropped it on the counter beside his struggling coffee machine. The less than peak-performing machine was what commanded all of his attention at the moment. Gurgling, it gave every indication that it was just about in its last throes of life.

None of his coffeemakers were long-lived and he'd been through this before. Alex judged that he'd probably have to buy a new coffeemaker sometime in the latter half of next week—if not sooner. As a rule, he hated to shop, but this was more important than his dislike for standing in a checkout line. He could function fairly well with little to no sleep and a lot of other things, but he couldn't function at all without that first cup of coffee in the morning.

Usually followed by a second cup—and a third if he was skipping breakfast.

The newspaper was part of his morning ritual, as well. Not that he usually had time to read it. Most days he took off a couple of minutes after he brought the paper into the apartment. Like so many of his under-thirty-five generation, most—if not all—of his news came from the internet. And, on occasion, from the radio he listened to while driving in to work.

Still, he wouldn't dream of terminating his newspaper subscription. He considered it a tragedy that the written word was dying out. A great many newspapers around the country had already permanently closed their doors, ending, in his opinion, a fine old tradition. He was not about to add to that and help bury that longtime industry by withdrawing his support from the local Aurora paper. Though basically not an optimist, he did still hang on to the very clichéd belief that every little bit helped.

Alex had a soft spot in his heart for newspapers. He always had. For a while, when he was about ten or so, he had delivered newspapers to people's doorsteps in an attempt to earn some money of his own.

Honest money.

Even then, honest money had been a rarity in his family.

But he'd tried.

Alex poured himself a travel mug's worth of thick black liquid, guaranteed to wake up every fiber of his body whether he wanted it to or not. The people he worked with in the department claimed it could probably also be used to fix the cracks in the street asphalt.

Preoccupied, he wound up filling the mug too high. Some of the coffee escaped as he screwed on the top of the mug. Slipping down the sides of the steel-gray thermos, the black liquid began leaking onto the front page of the newspaper.

Swallowing a few choice words that normally didn't get voiced until he was already a couple of hours into his shift, Alex reached for the dish towel hanging off the handle on his stove.

With quick movements he tried to wipe away the coffee before it blurred the front headline.

Which was when he read the words.

And how he wound up reading the article instead of leaving for work right at that point.

The headline that fairly screamed across the front page this morning was about a robbery. Specifically, a break-in in one of Aurora's high-end developments. Apparently, according to the journalist covering the local story, it was the third such robbery of its kind in a short period. The owners of the house had been away in Europe and returned to find that their priceless art collection had been stolen.

Nothing else had been taken.

Alex read the article from start to finish, carefully taking in every word. A wave of nausea came over him as he read.

"Oh God," he muttered under his breath as he came to the end of the article, no more reassured now than he had been when he'd started reading. "This isn't you, is it?"

The question was addressed to a man who was not there.

Alex's voice, and the question he'd asked, echoed about his small kitchen, haunting him with the possible implications.

Alex tossed the newspaper back on the counter. This was supposed to be behind him, he angrily thought.

Who are you kidding? It's never going to be behind you.

The words, coming from deep inside him, taunted Alex.

The pinched, sick feeling he had been experiencing in the pit of his stomach accompanied him all the way to the precinct.

With luck, he'd catch a case and be distracted.

Alex crossed his fingers.

Chapter 1

Brian Cavanaugh, chief of detectives of the Aurora Police Department, was well aware of the very fine line that existed between nepotism and utilizing the right person for the right job. He'd walked that line countless times since assuming his present position.

To his own satisfaction, he had never been guilty of nepotism, although there were those who would swear differently. They were the ones whose potential did not measure up to the job and they found it easier to point fingers and complain than to undertake the hard work of evaluating and improving themselves.

Brian didn't much care when the insults, born of bruised egos, were directed at him. After all his years on the force and in this chair, he'd become used to fielding the ones that needed to be dealt with and ignoring the ones that would die of their own accord. But he was always extra judicious because he did mind if the person he was singling out for a special assignment came under fire through no actual fault of his or her own, other than having the same surname as he did.

Granted there were a great many Cavanaughs spread through the different divisions within the police force, but as a rule, Cavanaughs worked twice as hard as the person beside them to do the job and prove that they had earned the right to be where they were. Not a single Cavanaugh had ever been promoted without first demonstrating that he or she not only had the necessary potential to do the job— whatever it might be—but also knew how to use it.

As was the case with the blonde, blue-eyed patrol officer who was currently standing, looking somewhat uneasy, before him in his office.

"You can sit, you know, Officer Cavanaugh," he told the young woman.

"If you don't mind, sir, I'd like to stand."

Standing made Valri Cavanaugh feel just a little more in control and slightly less vulnerable than if she were sitting, although in this particular situation, the petite blonde had a feeling that the nervousness wouldn't abate even if she were hanging from the ceiling like a circus trapeze artist.

"I don't mind," Brian assured her in his easy, deep baritone voice. "But if you're worried, I can guarantee that there won't be any need for a quick getaway on your part."

In response, Valri offered him a quick, somewhat embarrassed smile and then slowly lowered herself into one of the two chairs situated before his desk.

He couldn't help noticing that his cousin Murdoch's youngest daughter made contact with the seat as if she were anticipating being forcefully propelled out of it at any second. In what he could only assume was an attempt for stability, he observed her fingers wrapping around each of the armrests in what looked to be a death grip.

Her attention, however, appeared to be focused entirely on him.

"Do you know why I asked to see you, Officer Cavanaugh?" he asked gently, although ever mindful of the positions that separated them. Privately, he was family, but professionally, he was the chief of detectives and her ultimate superior. It was as the chief of Ds that he was presently speaking to this unusually gifted officer.

"No, sir," Valri answered honestly, then added, the corners of her mouth curving ever so slightly, "but I think it might have something to do with computers."

"It not only 'might' have something to do with computers, it most definitely does. The head of the computer lab recently brought your considerable skills to my attention."

It was a known fact that the head of the computer lab was an absolute wizard with computers. She was also Brenda Cavanaugh, married to Detective Dax Cavanaugh and one of the chief's daughters-in-law.

"She said that you were invaluable, taking on some of the overflow from her desk last month. She also mentioned that you recently helped get the goods on those two women who were killing senior citizens."

The case had been an involved one that seemingly had no connection at first. These were older people with no families who were dying from what at first appeared to be heart attacks. After some considerable cyberdigging, it turned out that each of these people had crossed paths with two seemingly kindly volunteers who ingratiated themselves to the senior citizens and offered to take out and pay for insurance policies that would cover all their funeral expenses when the time came. The time, for all of them once they signed on the dotted line, came a lot quicker than anticipated.

One of the investigating detectives, Duncan Cavanaugh, had prevailed on his younger sister to do a little virtual research and she had been the one who had uncovered the insurance fraud.

"I'm glad I could help, sir," Valri murmured, wondering where all this was going.

She had already met the man sitting behind the oak desk a number of times at her granduncle Andrew's house. Tall, distinguished with a touch of gray at his temples, the man inspired loyalty and respect. She knew that he was always ready to listen, but she wouldn't have dreamed of being informal with him in his office. This was the job. It required that she be a consummate professional in every way. The last thing she would have wanted was for the chief of Ds to think she was trying to cash in on the fact that she was a Cavanaugh and related to him.

Suddenly finding out that there was a large branch of the family in Aurora had motivated her to apply for the police department here instead of remaining where she was, on the force in Shady Canyon, the city she had grown up in. But she hadn't done that with the idea of advancement foremost in her mind.

She'd also come here because she wanted to get to know her relatives better. After all, it wasn't every day that a person discovered there was a whole cache of relatives less than fifty miles away whose paths had never crossed their own.

"CSI Cavanaugh tells me that you're quick and extremely good at what you do," Brian went on, referring to his daughter-in-law. Brian watched the young officer closely as he spoke.

She didn't preen in response to the praise, which was in her favor, he thought.

"She was being kind," Valri told him.

While she loved being appreciated and complimented, those were the very things that also caused Valri to fidget somewhat. She never knew quite what to say when she was on the receiving end of merited praise.

"Yes, CSI Cavanaugh is kind," Brian agreed. "But at the same time, she makes a point of being very accurate. Being in a league of her own, she is not impressed easily. And you, Officer Cavanaugh, impressed her, which is enough for me."

"Enough, sir?" Valri clearly didn't understand what the chief meant by that.

"Hunter Rogers was found dead in his apartment this morning," Brian told her, then asked, "Is that name familiar to you?"

She knew the name and the man. There'd been a time when her sphere of interest had been completely different from what it was now. Now her life was all about law enforcement and family. Then it had been the captivating and addictive world of gaming. In leaving that world behind, Valri felt she had definitely traded upward.

"He's a gamer, sir. Rogers makes—made," she corrected, taking what the chief had just said into account, "his living taking on challengers in competitions around the country. He was always the one to beat," she added. "In the last year, he more or less disappeared off the grid. He's dead?" she questioned, surprised. She would have expected the man to have turned up playing in some tournament, not this.

Brian nodded. "He was murdered." The case, only a few hours old, had come to his attention rather quickly. Moreover, his gut told him that there was more to this than just possibly an argument that had gone wrong. "Turns out that he might have been a little bit more than just a gamer."

"What do you mean, sir?" Valri asked.

Brian noticed that the young officer was no longer clutching the armrests, nor was she perched on the edge of her seat, ready to take off. Her whole body appeared to be focused on what he was telling her.

"Rogers was shot from behind and whoever did it also smashed his laptop."

Now her interest was really aroused. Uncooperative computers had a way of igniting tempers like nothing else could. She'd known people who'd lost their tempers with computers to such an extent that they'd punched the keyboard or thrown their laptop on the floor, but this sounded as if there had been more involved than a flash of temper.

"Smashed, sir?" she asked, hoping he would dole out a few more details describing what had been involved in this murder/machine-icide he was informing her about.

Brian sat back in his chair, telling the young

woman he'd summoned the details he'd been given so far.

"The detective on the scene said it looked as if a sledgehammer had been taken to it. Someone apparently wanted to get rid of whatever was on that computer. The quickest way would have probably been to take the laptop with them and then wipe out the hard drive, but I'm guessing whoever did it didn't want to take a chance on being caught with Rogers's computer." Brian watched her expression as he gave Valri his theory. "And I'd assume that taking a sledgehammer to a laptop pretty much renders it a total loss."

"Not every time," she told the chief, choosing her words carefully. It wasn't something she was accustomed to doing. For the most part, she talked to coworkers and friends, not superiors, and while she didn't babble, there was always an unbridled enthusiasm to her tone. One that she was consciously restraining.

Brian looked at her with interest. "Oh? So the information on the hard drive wasn't completely destroyed?"

"There might still be data that can be lifted," she told him. She didn't want to raise the chief's hopes too high, but at the same time, there was a very small chance that all was not lost. "It depends on how hard the hammer came down on the laptop, the angle it hit, things like that."

It was a whole new world out there than when he had been this officer's age, Brian thought, silently marveling at what he was hearing. "You mean that the data might be retrievable?"

"Not all of it," she was quick to qualify, again not to raise his hopes too high. "But it's conceivable that a little here and there might have been spared and could still be gathered—but it won't be easy," she warned.

"Nothing worthwhile ever is," Brian said, more of an aside than as a direct comment. "If I gave you the laptop to look over, do you think that you might be able to extract the data—provided that it *can* be extracted?" he added.

Brian wanted the young officer to know that there was no pressure attached to the directive. He didn't expect miracles. But if there was one to be had, from what he had been told, he felt that she was the one to pull it off.

Valri took in a deep breath before answering. "I'd do my best, sir," she told him.

"Can't ask for anything more than that," he told her. "Officer Cavanaugh, I'm going to pull you off your present assignment and set you up with a desk and a computer in Homicide."

"Homicide?" she repeated, surprised. She had just assumed that if the chief wanted her to do tech work, that her desk would be down in the computer lab, where the rest of the CSI unit was located along with all of its specialized equipment.

"That's where the case initially landed. The man *is* dead," Brian reminded her.

"Right." For a second, focusing on what the chief was saying about the laptop, the homicide had slipped her mind. Valri cleared her throat, which drew the chief's attention to her. "If you don't mind my asking, sir," she interjected.

"Ask any question you want, Officer Cavanaugh," he told her. "This is the time to clear things up."

She knew that he really didn't have to answer this. Law enforcement agents had the luxury of deflecting questions by saying that the answer would compromise an ongoing investigation. It was an all-purpose excuse that cast shadows on any beams of light that might be attempting to squeeze their way out.

But she knew she at least had to make the attempt to find out the basics here.

"What is it about this gamer, about Hunter Rogers, that makes his laptop important enough for you to try to get it resurrected?" It had to involve something other than his gaming strategies, but what?

"Turns out that Rogers wasn't just a gamer, he was a hacker," Brian told her. "And as for his laptop, we're trying to find out if something on there got him killed—or possibly, might get someone else killed." At present, he had no idea what they were up against, and it frustrated him no end. He didn't like operating blindly.

Valri watched the chief. "You're thinking that whoever killed Hunter knew what was on his laptop and what? Decided to save the world from it?"

"Not exactly," he corrected her misconception. "We're thinking that whoever killed Rogers wants to use whatever is on the computer and doesn't want to share that information with the rest of the class." He spread his wide palms on top of his desk blotter and leaned slightly forward for a better look into her eyes. He found a good many of his answers there when he spoke to people. "So, Officer Cavanaugh, are you up for this?"

Valri could barely sit still and contain the energy that she felt surging through her. "I love a challenge, sir."

Brian smiled, nodding his head. He'd made the right call. "So I've heard."

"Where is the laptop now, sir?" Valri wanted to know.

"Temporarily, it's still locked up down in Homicide," Brian told her. "Detective Brody has custody of it at the moment. Are you acquainted with Detective Alex Brody?" he asked.

The name was vaguely familiar, but she had no idea why. Most likely she'd overheard it being mentioned by one of the other uniforms. In any case, she had no personal recollection of the man.

Valri shook her head. "No, sir."

"Well, you will be. I'm having the two of you partner up for this case. Temporarily," he added on.

"He's good with computers, too?" she asked, assuming that was why the chief was putting the two of them together.

Brian laughed rather heartily in response to her question. Valri had her answer before the chief opened his mouth and said a word.

"Not to hear him tell it. But Detective Brody *is* good with people and he's a damn fine detective to boot." He could see by the look on his younger cousin's face that she was trying to follow his reasoning and she wasn't succeeding. "I'm putting the two of you out in the field together," he explained. "You'll each supply strengths that the other is lacking."

"Won't Detective Brody feel resentful, being paired up with a beat cop?" she asked. She wasn't a rookie, but she had a feeling that Brody would think of her in that light.

"Possibly," Brian acknowledged. "Which is why I'm issuing you a temporary promotion to detective for the duration of this investigation."

"Promotion? To detective?" she repeated in an awed whisper, never taking her eyes off the chief. "Seriously, sir?"

Valri was certain that at any second now, he'd come back to his senses, say he'd made a mistake and apologize just before he told her that she was going to remain a patrol officer.

"You have a problem with that, Officer Cavanaugh?" he asked her in all seriousness.

"What? Oh no, sir. No, I don't. It's just that—" Her words all but evaporated as her voice trailed off into something that sounded like a squeak.

"It's just that...?" he repeated, waiting for her to finish her sentence.

She had to be honest with him. Yes, she had joined the police force with dreams of eventually making detective. But even in her wildest dreams, it took some time to get there. She'd been on the force only a little over two years.

"I didn't expect to have it happen so fast," she finally said.

A comfortable as well as comforting smile slipped over his lips. "Life happens fast, Officer Cavanaugh. We have to try to keep up. And besides, the promotion is temporary, not permanent," he reminded her. "At least, not yet," he added with an encouraging note in his voice. "But it's been my experience that as a whole, Cavanaughs are a very tough bunch to keep down." His eyes held hers. "I'd like to believe that the same can be said for you."

"Yes, sir," Valri replied with conviction, beaming. The next second, she realized that it probably sounded to the chief as if she was bragging so she made an attempt to backtrack and say something a bit more humble. "I mean, I'm not trying to get you to think that I—"

"One thing you will learn, Officer," Brian said, raising his voice and cutting through her statement, "is that no one 'gets' me to think anything."

"No, sir," she responded quickly, then realized that she was interrupting him while he was talking. "I mean—sorry, sir."

"Nothing to be sorry about, Officer. And I'm proud to say that I've never been known to bite a single officer, so relax, Officer Cavanaugh."

"Easier said than done, sir."

He laughed then at the simple truth she had uttered in desperation.

"Yes, I imagine that it is," he agreed with a soft chuckle. "So, tell me—and think carefully—are you up for this?" he asked her again.

There was no hesitation in Valri's voice this time as she gave him her answer. "Yes, sir."

He nodded, pleased.

"Good." And then he hit the button on his intercom, connecting him to his administrative assistant out front. "You can send him in now, Raleigh," he told the woman who had once patrolled the streets of Aurora, along with Lila, his wife.

"Right away, sir," the feminine voice on the intercom promised.

The next moment, the door to Brian's inner office was being opened and a tall, broad-shouldered detective with dirty-blond hair that was slightly longer than regulation dictated came walking in as if he owned every square inch of space he passed.

Sparing an appreciative glance at the officer sitting in front of the chief of Ds—Brody was not one who didn't take note of beauty wherever he came in contact with it—the detective then focused his attention entirely on the man who he'd been told had requested his presence in his office.

Alex had spent his morning with a dead man in a dingy apartment that desperately needed a thorough cleaning and a massive dose of fresh air. The chief's immaculate, spacious office was a very welcome contrast.

Alex stood behind the only empty chair in the room, waiting to find out if this was going to be something he needed to sit down for, or if this was just a quick, "touch base" sort of a meeting.

"You sent for me, sir?" he asked the chief.

Brian smiled. Gesturing for the young detective to sit down, he said, "I did indeed, Detective Brody."

Chapter 2

"Detective Brody, this is Officer Valri Cavanaugh," Brian told the new arrival. "Officer Cavanaugh, this is Alexander Brody, the homicide detective who caught the case we were discussing."

Alex nodded at the woman to his left. Surprised when she put out her hand to him, he shook it belatedly, then glanced back at the chief.

"One of yours, sir?"

He'd put it in the form of a question, but the query was obviously rhetorical in nature. It was a given that *all* the Cavanaughs were related to each other in one way or another. It was one of the first things he'd learned when he came out of the academy and joined the Aurora PD.

The second thing he'd learned was that having all these related people around him was not really such a bad thing. The ones he had encountered so far—especially the detectives he'd worked with—were all at the top of their game.

The chief gave him an indulgent smile. "You're all 'one of mine,' Detective," Brian informed him.

Coming from anyone else, the words might have sounded a bit patronizing, but because of everything he'd heard—and his own limited experience with the man—the chief of Ds actually meant that. Brian Cavanaugh had been around for quite a while and he regarded everyone on the force as part of his extended family.

And, like a family, members were to be kept safe whenever possible, and when it became necessary, they all pulled together to get the job done and protect their own. Anything short of that was deemed unacceptable.

The funny thing was, Alex knew for a fact that nearly everyone tried to live up to those standards to the very best of their ability.

"Sorry, sir," Alex apologized to the chief. "I meant no disrespect."

"None taken," Brian replied. "Let's get down to business," he continued, drawing his chair in closer and leaning forward over his desk. "Lieutenant Latimore tells me that you caught the last case."

"Are you referring to the gamer who was found

dead this morning?" Alex asked, wanting to be completely certain that he and the chief were talking about the same murder. When the chief nodded, Alex confirmed what the man already knew. "Yes, sir, that's mine."

Brian had one last piece of information he wanted to verify before going ahead with his plan. "Lieutenant Latimore also told me that your partner's currently laid up in the hospital."

Alex nodded. The incident was only a week in the past. "Detective Montgomery had a slight difference of opinion with a suspect driving a Jeep Cherokee SUV. The suspect thought he'd win the argument by running my partner over."

"As I recall, you shot him from quite a distance. Most people play it safe and go for a kill shot from that far away, but you didn't," Brian said.

"He can't talk if he's dead, sir," Alex told him simply.

"Very true," Brian agreed. His eyes never left the detective's. "Detective, I'm going to be giving you a temporary partner for this assignment."

"Yes, sir," Alex replied stoically.

He was trying his best to have his mouth offer at least a half smile, but he wasn't quite succeeding at the moment. He was having better luck at steeling himself for what he sensed was going to be a bomb landing squarely on him.

Brian laughed softly. "It's a temporary partnership, Detective. Not a life sentence," Brian told the detective. "Loosen up a little."

"Of course, sir," Alex answered, struggling to restrain his uptight feeling, or at the very least, to keep it from showing. But he had worked long and hard to get to this position within the police force. He hadn't done it to be turned into what, in his book, amounted to a glorified babysitter.

He slanted another, longer look at the officer sitting in the other chair. Even though she was in uniform, wearing her dress blues, she still seemed more like a cheerleader playing dress-up for Halloween than an actual police officer.

Judging by her face alone, he wouldn't have said that she was actually old enough to be wearing the uniform. But she had to be, right? He sincerely doubted that the chief would have bent the rules and gotten her into the academy if she were underage. That wasn't the kind of thing that Brian Cavanaugh would do.

Besides, that sort of thing was out of the chief's hands, as far as he knew.

Still, none of that changed the fact that he felt as if he were being asked to supervise a totally wet-behind-the-ears beat cop.

Alex had never been the kind of man who stewed about something in private until it all but exploded inside him. Though restraint was his first order of business, if there was something he couldn't docilely accept, the thought of registering a complaint was not beyond him. He didn't want to rock the boat—this was the first professional interaction he'd had with the chief—but he wasn't about to meekly accept the situation without a few facts.

"Could I ask why, sir?"

"Why what?"

"Why me?" Alex asked bluntly, for once not relying exclusively on his ability to charm people. The chief, he well knew, was a man who appreciated directness.

Brian paused for a long moment, studying both his cousin and the young detective. "You mean why am I saddling you with someone who is completely green when it comes to being out in the field as a detective?" Brian asked.

"Not exactly in those words," Alex replied a tad uneasily, aware that the officer was looking at him intently. "But, well, yes. I'm really not much good at teaching anyone anything."

It wasn't modesty that prompted the disclaimer but rather honesty. He knew his strengths, of which he felt he had many, and his weaknesses. Mentoring or, more bluntly, teaching was among the latter.

The chief's mouth curved ever so minutely. "Actually, I thought that Detective Cavanaugh—" he glanced toward his niece and saw that she brightened at the sound of her new title "—might be able to teach *you* a few things."

Alex blinked. Now he was *really* lost.

"Sir?" Alex asked, requesting an explanation for that last statement.

"You're dealing with a dead gamer who, I'm told, was also rather a well-known and proficient hacker. Both professions, from all indications, do not promote lasting friendships. It's more of a case of the exact opposite being true. A lot of people hated this man's guts. His ego, his bravado, all that made Hunter Rogers a walking target.

"I want to find out who decided to indulge in target practice and *why*. I also want to find out if Rogers's laptop can be salvaged."

There, at least, he could offer the chief some definitive information—or so he believed. "Only if you're interested in hanging on to a very unique doorstop," Alex told him.

The moment the words were out of his mouth, he knew what he'd just said was wrong. The look on the chief's face said as much.

"You and I see it that way," Brian said. "But that's where Detective Cavanaugh comes in." He gestured toward her. "She thinks that there might be something that can be saved on that laptop."

Alex remained unconvinced and he shook his head, contradicting what the chief had just said.

"No way," Alex said firmly, then turned toward the woman and said, "No offense, Officer, but I saw it and you didn't. That thing is now just a thin, broken waffle."

Her interest fully engaged, she wasn't about to let the detective stand in her way. "Then you won't mind me looking it over."

Alex shrugged. He knew when fighting city hall was useless. And this was one of those times. "Hey, knock yourself out. Look all you want. You still won't find anything." He turned back toward Brian. "It's a waste of time, sir."

"Duly noted, Detective," Brian replied in a tone of voice that told Alex the chief still intended to have this pseudo-detective take a look at it.

Well, it was her time to waste, Alex supposed. And if she was busy playing detective and attempting to resurrect that wreck of a laptop, well, then, she wouldn't be getting underfoot and in his way, would she? And, if for some remote reason she *did* find a scrap of viable information on the laptop, so much the better. Alex saw it as a win-win situation.

"Take her up to Homicide," Brian instructed the detective. "I've given permission for Detective Cavanaugh to take over a desk and a computer. She'll be using Montgomery's for the time being, until he gets back," he told Alex.

"And then what, sir?" Alex asked. He wasn't one to plan too far ahead, but he did believe in having something in place against a future that didn't treat slackers kindly.

"Well, by then I expect you and Detective Cavanaugh to have the murder solved," Brian informed him in a voice that could be described only as confident. "That'll be all for now," he told the duo, dismissing them. "Oh, and Detective?"

Both he and the cheerleader he'd been saddled with said "Yes?" at the exact same moment. Alex did his best not to appear annoyed.

Brian smiled at the stereo response. "Keep me posted," he instructed before getting back to reviewing the report that was currently on his desk.

"Yes, sir," Alex replied, trying not to clench his jaw too hard.

"Absolutely!" Valri declared happily.

Alex suppressed a sigh. It was going to be a very *long* investigation.

As they left the outer office and went into the hall to get the elevator, Valri found she was having trouble containing a surge of enthusiasm.

"This is exciting," she announced, feeling as if her feet were barely touching the ground. Just this morning, she'd been wondering how long it would take her to work her way up to detective, and now here she was, trying the role on for size. It just did not get any better than this.

Reaching the elevator half a step before Alex did, she pressed the up arrow and continued talking to her new partner.

"I mean, it's not exciting for Hunter. He's dead.

But this is going to be my first case." That wasn't quite accurate, so she backtracked a little. "Well, my first case that I get to *solve*. All the other times, I just got to be there at the start, putting up yellow tape, taking notes, then handing them over to the detectives who took the case."

She was fairly floating as she continued, taking no notice of the fact that there was no feedback coming from her tall, dark blond, handsome green-eyed partner.

The elevator car arrived, opening its doors slowly.

"But this time around, I get to *be* a detective. God, I hope I don't screw up," she said as she got into the elevator car.

"That makes two of us," Alex said under his breath. He hadn't intended for her to hear, but she did. Rather than insult her, it seemed to reinforce what she was thinking.

"You can tell me when I'm out of line," Valri told him. Then, as if he'd said something to decline this request, she went on to assure him that criticizing her would be all right. "I'm the youngest in my family and I'm used to being criticized, so you won't hurt my feelings."

Right now, hurting this effervescent officer's feelings was the furthest thing from his mind. "Good to know."

If she heard the sarcasm in his voice, she gave no indication.

"Have you been a detective long?" she asked as the doors again opened on the fifth floor and she fairly bounced out of the elevator.

He spared her a glance. "Longer than you."

Again, Valri didn't appear to take any offense at his tone. "Everyone's been a detective longer than I have," she said with a laugh that he would have thought was charming if he wasn't currently being so annoyed at the spot he found himself in.

It wasn't that he resented getting a new partner, temporarily or otherwise. He'd had a couple already, and besides, it was the chief's prerogative to pair up anyone he wanted. But what he *did* resent was the unspoken instruction that he needed to watch over this chattering blue-eyed blonde magpie and make sure that he returned her to the chief at the end of this assignment in the same condition that he'd received her.

That meant he couldn't strangle her.

Granted, this energized temporary detective was very easy on the eyes, and in another scenario he might have even made a play for her. Beautiful women were a weakness for him even though he changed them a little more frequently than he had his jackets dry-cleaned.

But this wasn't another scenario, it was *this* scenario and she was a Cavanaugh, which, drop-dead gorgeous or not, meant hands off unless, of course, he wanted to risk *losing* those same hands.

The moment he walked into the Homicide Division with her, he saw heads turning in their direction. If he didn't know better, he would have said it was as if they'd tripped some sort of an invisible wire that immediately set off a silent alarm, heard only by the other homicide detectives who populated the squad room.

Heads turned and conversations slowly died out. Alex knew they weren't looking at him. It was a given that news traveled approximately at the speed of light around the building.

If he hadn't already figured it out before, he could see now that his new albatross wasn't shy. Leaving his side for the moment, she worked the room, waving and saying "hi" to just about everyone and, from all appearances, schmoozing with various people in the department.

Detective Albatross was probably related, in one way or another, to all of them. Which meant that all eyes would be on them—and on him—to see if they were doing a good job.

If *he* was doing a good job mentoring her.

This was going to be a challenge, Alex thought grudgingly. A definite challenge for him, both as a detective and as a man. He would have to be sharp as the former and very hands-off as the latter.

The first part was not going to be nearly as much of a challenge as the second.

He waited as Valri made the various rounds

through the room. He didn't bother calling her over or saying anything to her until she finally rejoined him.

"I didn't realize there were so many Cavanaughs in Homicide," she told him.

"Murder attracts them, I guess," he quipped. "Now, if you're finished playing homecoming queen, I'll show you where your desk is."

"Brody, are you annoyed with me for some reason?" she asked, following him.

"What possible reason could I have to be annoyed with you?" he asked sarcastically, thinking that would put her off for a little while.

He should have known better.

"I don't know. That's why I'm asking," she told him.

"I'm not annoyed," he lied. "Just preoccupied."

"With the case?" she asked.

He bit his tongue and gave her the appropriate answer, not the real one. "Yeah, with the case."

She turned her face up to him and smiled. "Then let's get started."

He couldn't strangle her here—or even vent. There were too many witnesses. All he could do was mentally shrug and let it go.

Alex brought her over to his desk. Butted against it was Jake Montgomery's desk. The contrast between the two work surfaces was like night and day.

When it came to neatness, Alex was definitely

not a stickler, but his desk looked like the last word in tidiness when compared with Montgomery's. His partner's desk had been officially dubbed no-man's land the first week the guy had taken it over. Alex used to say that Montgomery never met a scrap of paper he didn't like.

He had no idea how Montgomery could lay his hands on reports when he needed them, but the man could and he did, each and every time. Alex figured that a little bit of magic was involved, but he asked no questions, afraid of the answer he might get.

Now that he thought of it, the very sight of Montgomery's desk might make this pseudo-detective turn tail and run.

"That's your desk," he told Valri, gesturing at the piece of office furniture hidden beneath piles and piles of papers, files and old candy wrappers. "Computer's right there—somewhere," he added since at the moment, the laptop that Montgomery was using just before he landed in the hospital was not visible.

His guess was that it had to be buried somewhere beneath all the various documents.

Valri stood in front of Montgomery's desk, stunned. She was definitely not a neatness freak, but this was a whole different ball game. She glanced toward her partner to see if he was putting her on. But he looked dead serious.

"How can you tell?" she asked Alex, eyeing the disaster area.

The papers were all precariously stacked and she had a feeling that if she tried to remove so much as a single page, an avalanche would result. Maybe this was some sort of a prank that was religiously played on the "new kid" on the block. She glanced in Alex's direction, hoping to be proved right.

His expression gave nothing away.

"Easy. I remember seeing it there just before he wound up in the hospital. He used it every day," Alex told her.

Valri squared her shoulders. "Okay. If you say so," she said as she began to feel around in the general vicinity, spreading her long, graceful fingers beneath the scattered papers.

Alex thought it would take her a while to locate the laptop, but he hadn't counted on the fact that like most of her family, Valri was born with a stubborn streak that wouldn't allow her to give up. It had her tackling each challenge as if she was competing for first place in a marathon. Nothing less would do.

Within a few minutes, she was grinning broadly, her eyes all but dancing as she glanced up at Alex. He found himself wishing that she looked more like his absent partner than a beauty pageant winner— bubbly, with a flawless complexion and what looked to be killer curves beneath her clothes. His partner was 0 for 3 in that department. "You're right," she cried, sounding as if she had just located buried treasure rather than an MIA laptop. "It's right here."

Almost in slow motion, Valri extracted the laptop from beneath a pile of papers, careful not to dislodge any of the documents.

To Alex's surprise, she actually managed to do it, leaving the stacks upon stacks of papers almost exactly the way they were.

And then, as she held up the laptop for his benefit and her own delight, it happened. As if the piles of papers had been set on a ten-second delay timer, suddenly the less than well-ordered stacks began to fall, fast and furious, to the floor right before her feet.

And *on* her feet, as well.

Within seconds, there was an entire off-white mountain of papers engulfing her practically up to her knees.

Chapter 3

"Brody, what're you trying to do, lose another partner before she even gets started by burying her alive in Montgomery's useless garbage?"

The sharply voiced question came from behind Alex. He didn't have to turn around to know who the gravelly voice belonged to. Only one person in the squad room talked like that. Len Latimore, the lieutenant who had recently taken over the Homicide Division, had a voice that sounded as if he had spent the past twenty-nine days drinking hard liquor that went down anything but smoothly.

"I'm not trying to bury her, Len," Alex said, although now that he thought of it, that didn't sound like altogether a bad idea. "She was trying to locate

Montgomery's laptop, which was supposed to be in there somewhere."

Of medium height and build, and appearing as if he were permanently rumpled, Latimore scowled as he circumvented the off-white avalanche around the newest addition to the division.

"Looks like she found a lot more than that." If there was anything Latimore hated, it was clutter not of his own making. "Get a large box out of the supply room and clean this stuff up," he instructed.

"Yes, sir," Valri responded. She'd just assumed, since she was low woman on the totem pole and, after all, she had been the one to disrupt the precarious stacks in the first place, that the lieutenant was talking to her. "Which way is the supply room?" she asked.

"Not you," Latimore snapped. "You, I want to see in my office. You—" he turned to face Alex "—can get all of Montgomery's junk cleared away."

"Montgomery's going to want all this when he gets back," Alex pointed out. It wasn't that he was particularly fond of the mess that his partner made, but he knew how he would have felt if someone had come and moved all of his things while he was in the hospital, especially since he'd been put there by job-related injuries.

"Yeah, well, what he wants and what he gets are two damn different things. This isn't his squad room, it's mine, and I don't want to see this when I come out again," he warned, pointing to all the papers scattered on the floor around the chief's cousin. "Do I make myself clear?"

"It's my fault, sir." Valri was quick to speak up. "I caused the papers to fall."

The last thing she wanted was for this to cause any hard feelings between her and Brody. She might still be green, but she knew that wasn't the way to start a new partnership, temporary or otherwise.

Latimore's frown deepened. "I'm not talking about whose 'fault' it is, Cavanaugh. I'm talking about cleanup.

"In my office, Cavanaugh," Latimore ordered gruffly. "Now."

Valri had no choice but to do as she was told. She couldn't risk getting the lieutenant any angrier than he already seemed to be. Otherwise, she would have remained to help clean up the blizzard of pages before she went into the short, bull of a man's office.

Valri glanced over her shoulder at her partner. She fervently hoped that the detective wouldn't hold this against her. He didn't look overly thrilled to be working with her to begin with. Having to clean up a mess she had caused, accidentally or not, was only going to make matters worse.

She was acutely aware of garnering covert glances as she followed the lieutenant to his office.

Reaching the glass-enclosed lair that looked barely larger than a small walk-in closet, Latimore waited impatiently until she had crossed the threshold. The second she did, he closed the door behind her.

He walked to his desk and sat down, waving at the chair that faced him and expecting her to take the hint. When she didn't, he ordered, "Sit," as if he were training a dog. Rumor had it that Latimore was better with dogs than he was with people.

Valri didn't remember bending her knees and dropping into the chair, but she must have because the next moment, she was sitting and uneasily facing the lieutenant.

All but holding her breath, she waited for the man to speak.

Not one for being delicate or standing on ceremony, Latimore got right down to the question he wanted resolved.

"You got any trouble looking at dead people?"

For a moment, the question caught her completely off guard. Of all the things she had anticipated that Latimore could ask her, this was _not_ one of them.

"I don't know," Valri answered honestly after a beat. "I've never looked at a dead person."

Latimore grunted. He didn't look as if he was satisfied with her answer. "How long have you been on the force?"

"A little more than two years, sir."

"And in all that time, you never saw a dead homicide victim?" he questioned skeptically.

"No, sir. I've dealt with a couple of victims who had been shot, but they were still alive. Mostly," she enumerated quickly for his benefit, "I've dealt with break-ins, home invasions and robberies."

"How do you *think* you'll react to seeing a dead body?" he asked.

She took a breath before answering. "It's not something I'd look forward to, but it's part of the job." And she was here to do her job.

Latimore looked far from satisfied, scowling at her. "Not answering my question, Cavanaugh. If you're going to fall apart, I need to know up front— like *now*," he emphasized, narrowing his eyes as he pinned her with them.

"I'm not going to fall apart because it *is* part of my job," she replied in a surprisingly calm manner, given her penchant for bubbliness. "I wouldn't be much good to Brody or the victim if I fell apart," she added. Not to mention that she would have felt that she was letting down a whole legion of Cavanaughs, both here and in Shady Canyon.

Latimore rocked back in his chair, which squeaked to signal the new position. His small brown eyes never left her face. "So you're telling me it's mind over matter for you, is that it?"

"Yes, sir."

The lieutenant surprised her with a quick, spasmodic smile as he nodded his approval. "Good. Oh, and one more thing."

So near and yet so far, she thought, all set to escape only to be pulled back. "Yes, sir?"

"That laptop that was found near the body, you really think you can get something off it?" There was genuine interest in his voice rather than any condescending note, tendering the notion that she was going to fail.

She tried to read the man in an effort to know what kind of answer he expected from her. If she said yes right off the bat, he'd undoubtedly think she was bragging and high on herself. So she couched her answer carefully. "I know I'd like to try."

"Yes or no, Cavanaugh. I don't have any time for your modesty or your aw-shucks routine. Give it to me straight. Can you do this?"

"Yes—probably," she tacked on. There were always problems that could crop up and she didn't want him berating her, or reminding her that she'd misrepresented herself and her abilities.

Latimore surprised her again by laughing in response. "I guess that'll just have to be good enough for now. Brody tends to like to work alone, so you're going to have to stay sharp in order to keep up and not get left behind."

Latimore made it sound as if Brody had never worked with anyone before. "But he had a partner," she protested.

"Montgomery usually handled the paperwork part of it—or mishandled it," the lieutenant tacked on, clearly not pleased with Montgomery's work ethic.

"I gathered that much," Valri said, unaware that her comment elicited a muffled laugh from the lieutenant that the man managed to hide.

"The one time they went into the field together, Montgomery wound up in the hospital," Latimore told her. "That made Brody more convinced than ever that he worked better alone. You're going to change that." It wasn't a comment, or a prediction, it was an order.

Was that her actual assignment? she couldn't help wondering. To get the detective to come around and get back into the swing of working with a partner? She supposed that she could do that.

"I'll give it a try, sir," Valri told the lieutenant.

"I don't want you to 'try,' I want you to 'do,'" he ordered in a no-nonsense voice. "Do I make myself clear, Cavanaugh?"

She squared her shoulders, every inch the consummate professional. "Crystal, sir."

Latimore nodded, satisfied—for now. "Good talk, Cavanaugh." He waved her out of the chair and out of the room. "Close the door on your way out."

He didn't have to tell her twice. Valri lost no time leaving.

When she got back to what was now her desk, Brody was still picking up the fallen files and haphazardly dumping them into a large rectangular box.

The box had held a six-month supply of paper for the printer ten minutes ago. The reams of paper were now stacked in a corner.

Without a word, Valri began picking up Montgomery's documents and depositing them into the box. Two could make the job go faster.

Alex raised his eyes for a moment. "So?" he asked as he got back to clearing the floor. He didn't bother organizing the papers. That was a job for Montgomery, not a man who valued his sanity.

Valri took a guess as to what her new partner was asking her. "The lieutenant wanted to officially welcome me into the office."

Alex stopped dumping pages for a moment and looked at her. The expression on his face told Valri that he didn't believe her.

What he said next confirmed it. "That man wouldn't 'officially welcome' the Three Wise Men if they came into the office." He frowned slightly as he got back to picking up papers. He tried not to notice that her close proximity was undermining his ability to concentrate. But then he'd always been an admirer of shapely limbs and a killer smile. It was nothing personal, he silently insisted. "We're not going to work well together if you lie to me, Cavanaugh."

She supposed it wouldn't hurt to level with him. After all, she hadn't done anything to merit the lieutenant's strange question to begin with. "He wanted to know if I got sick looking at dead bodies."

Alex laughed, nodding to himself. "Now *that* sounds like Latimore. Do you?" he asked her as a sidebar.

"I don't know." He glanced at her again, this time raising a skeptical eyebrow. She could see the question in his eyes. "It's what I told the lieutenant, too. I've never seen a dead body before."

There were times that he wished he could say that. "All the more reason for you to stay here, working on the smashed laptop, while I go and try to find some of the late Hunter Rogers's friends." Picking up the last of the papers, he tossed them into the box, which was now close to overflowing. "Speaking of which, do gamers even *have* friends?" he asked her out of sheer curiosity. To the best of his knowledge—having never had any interest in spending endless hours competing against people he didn't know—gamers were all a bunch of socially awkward, highly intellectual, obsessed-with-winning geeks.

"In a manner of speaking," Valri told him, then thought to expand her response. "I guess it all depends on your definition of *friends*."

That was easy. "Someone who knows all your secrets and still likes you."

The words had come to him automatically. It was something his father had once said to him.

By that definition, he himself had no friends, Alex thought. Because he had secrets he felt he couldn't—and thus didn't—share with anyone. Secrets that would create chasms between himself and the people he knew.

"If that's your criteria," Valri countered, "I guess what it comes down to is you actually define the word *likes*."

Alex blew out a breath. He was right. This world was a dog-eat-dog existence. "The gaming world doesn't sound very warm and friendly," he quipped.

"Well, that might be because it's not," she told him with an amused laugh. "It's all about competing and winning and coming up with a better game or, barring that, a better strategy."

"And you're part of all that?" he asked her.

Alex liked to think that he was a fair judge of people, and she didn't seem the type to enjoy that sort of bloodless, cutthroat competition. Nor did she seem the kind of person who liked spending time locked away, focused on a screen and annihilating the two-dimensional "enemy."

"I was," Valri acknowledged. "A long, long time ago, in another lifetime," she told him. "My horizons have become broadened since then, but I do like to keep my hand in the game every so often, just for practice," she admitted without any qualms, then added, "Keeps me on my toes."

"So would a pair of six-inch stilettos," he commented. Enough talk. He had to hit the streets and get cracking. "Okay, I'll have one of the uniforms sign out the smashed laptop from the evidence lockup and you see if you can resurrect the dead while I go back to Rogers's apartment and see if I can find something that'll lead me to one of his buddies—if he had any."

It hit her like a bolt out of the blue. "Randolph Wills," she called out to her partner's back as he was about to leave the squad room.

That stopped him in his tracks. Alex turned to look at her. He appeared somewhat skeptical at this sudden revelation. "What?"

"You said you wanted the name of one of Hunter's 'buddies.' Randolph Wills hung around him a lot, trying to absorb his technique as well as his expertise. He's kind of a leech, but his heart's in the right place."

"Most people's hearts can be found in the same place," he told her in an abrupt voice. "And you know this about Wills how?"

She made no attempt at building up the suspense. Instead, she told him point-blank, "Word of mouth." And then she smiled. She was leading him to a sunrise and his eyes were firmly shut. "The gaming community is both larger and smaller than you think."

Alex looked at her as if she had begun babbling gibberish. "Is that some kind of riddle for the ages?"

His sarcastic tone didn't faze her. Growing up as

the youngest had allowed her to be ready for *anything* and had given her a hide like a rhino. Her heart, though, was still her own and it was, for the most part, soft.

"Just a piece of information to contemplate," she told him with a smile. "And I really think that you're going to want me to go with you."

They had different definitions of the word *want*, he thought. And his definition had nothing to do with the job and everything to do with this gut reaction he was experiencing. If ever there was a "tread lightly" situation, this was it.

"And why is that?" Alex asked her.

"Well, for one thing I think I know where you can find Wills," she told him.

"And for another?" he asked because she clearly was building up to something.

"You're liable to need a translator," she told him, using the word *liable* out of consideration for the ego he had to have. Everyone was born with an ego and she had a feeling that his might be affected if what Wills told him—probably in a matter-of-fact voice—went straight over his head.

Alex was taking her words literally and he scowled. "He's foreign?"

"No, born right here in Silicon Valley," she attested, "but he might toss around terminology in his explanation that'll confuse you."

He wondered if she realized that she had just insulted him. "I'm not exactly a functioning illiterate."

"It has nothing to do with literacy, Brody," she assured him. "Gamers and hackers live in a different world from regular people—normal people if you will," she tacked on for his benefit. "I'm just saying that he might start tossing around terms that won't mean anything to you—and why should they? Gaming isn't your world."

She saw that her explanation didn't sit well with him. Most likely because she'd hurt his pride. She gave him a way out.

"Besides," she reminded him tactfully, "how can you be my mentor if I'm here in the office and you're out there in the field? How am I supposed to learn from you?"

Alex shrugged dismissively. "That wasn't my first thought," he told her.

Not to be put off, Valri suggested gently, "Maybe you can find a way to work it in."

She might look like a ball of fluff that was an easy pushover, but she was tenacious, he'd give her that. And he didn't feel like arguing the point. It wasted too much time.

"You want to come along that much, okay, fine. You're coming along," he told her, throwing in the towel for now. "Let's go."

"Can I drive?" she asked brightly, falling into step with him as he went into the hall.

"No." The single word was filled with finality, leaving absolutely no room for argument. Or so he believed.

"But I'm the one who knows the way," Valri pointed out.

He punched the down button on the wall, summoning the elevator car. "You also know how to talk—God *knows* you know how to talk," he said with a dramatic sigh. "That means that you can tell me how to get to Wills's place while I'm driving."

"It'd be easier if I just drove," she informed him a tad stubbornly.

That was *not* his definition of *easy*. Nothing about this exuberant, temporary detective was easy—and he'd bet his last dime that she knew it.

"That all depends on whose point of view you're looking at this from—yours, or mine," he told her. "And since it's my car, I win. You can still stay back in the office and play twenty-one pickup with the laptop, you know. Nobody's stopping you."

"I'll ride shotgun," she said, resigning herself to sitting in the passenger seat. She was not about to petulantly remain in the office because she didn't get her way.

"Nice of you to come around," Alex told her.

It was the first time since they had been introduced in the chief of Ds' office that she had seen her new partner smile.

She had an instant reaction to the smile, starting

with the very center of her stomach. If she didn't know better, she would have said that it had done a complete flip, spinning around a full 360 degrees and causing something akin to a tidal wave.

This man could very well be lethal, given the right set of circumstances.

It would be up to her to make sure that those circumstances never came together, at least not where she was concerned. She was here to learn, to advance, not be the target *for* advances.

Despite her wise words to the contrary, it took a while for her stomach to settle down.

Chapter 4

Buckling up, she gave Alex the gamer's address, then resisted the temptation to offer directions once he had pulled out of the parking lot and was on the main thoroughfare.

Since Brody was the native—or so she assumed—and she was the transplant, Valri figured that he knew the streets of Aurora far better than she did. Following that logic, she knew it was to her advantage *not* to offer a running commentary about distance, speed and the availability of shortcuts.

Even so, it was a temptation she had to do battle with, albeit silently. She'd learned long ago that men like Brody didn't enjoy following someone else's lead in any manner if they could help it. She'd seen that same trait manifested in her brothers, and while she could simply ignore it to her heart's content when it came to Brennan, Duncan, Bryce and Malloy, they were family and had to get along with her no matter what. That was just the Cavanaugh way: criticize all you want, but always be there for family when the chips were down.

Brody, on the other hand, could just up and dump her if the mood moved him, so she had to take care not to annoy him—at least not until they had a more secure partnership going. And she knew that nothing annoyed a man more than being given directions when they weren't asked for. For some reason that sort of thing was at the top of the list of things that seemed to threaten their manhood.

"You run out of words, Cavanaugh?" he asked her, curious as to what brought on this sudden, atypical silence. Alex glanced at the woman in the passenger seat to reassure himself that she hadn't fallen asleep for some reason. She hadn't. But she had been quiet for at least ten minutes. So far, from what he'd seen, that seemed out of character for her. Maybe if he knew what triggered it, he could use the information to cause her silence when he needed to.

As if deep in thought, Valri jumped in her seat at the sound of his voice. "What?"

"I asked if you ran out of words," he repeated.

"You're being quiet," he added by way of an explanation for his question.

Valri laughed shortly. "I didn't think you noticed."

"When the wall of noise suddenly just breaks apart like that, a person tends to notice." After all, she'd been talking almost nonstop before they got into his vehicle.

Valri shrugged. "I didn't want to get on your nerves."

If that had been her goal, she pretty much failed, Alex thought.

"Too late for that," he quipped. In case she was one of those overly sensitive types, he added something for her to focus on. "Let's just call this our 'get-acquainted period.'" Alex paused, letting that sink in.

Then, as if to live up to his word about getting acquainted, he asked her a question out of the blue. "Did they force you?"

Valri stared at the man whom fate and the chief had made her partner. Where had that come from? And what, exactly, was he asking her?

"Did who force me to do what?"

"Your family. Did they force you to become a cop?"

"No. Why would they?" Actually, Brennan as well as her father had tried to talk her out of it when they heard that she had decided to apply to the police academy.

Alex shrugged. "Well, every Cavanaugh I've run into or even heard of seems to be part of one division or other in the department. Even the one who isn't directly in law enforcement, that vet, I think her name is Patience, the police department has her down as the doctor on call for the K-9 unit in case any of them get hurt."

Valri offered a smile in exchange for his speculation. "I guess to serve and protect is just built into our DNA. I believe it's supposed to be a voluntary gene, though." Her teasing tone changed to one that was a little more serious. "Why would you think I had to be forced into joining law enforcement?"

"Because from what you said, you seemed to have other interests—interests that could have taken you in a completely different direction." The way, he couldn't help thinking, that his family's "occupation" could have taken him in, thereby drastically changing the direction of his life. "Besides, you look like you should be a cheerleader for some professional football team, not tackling would-be bad guys."

"Cheerleader, huh?" She seemed to roll that idea over in her mind. "Is that a compliment or a put-down?" she asked.

"It wasn't meant as either," he told her. "Definitely not a put-down. Why would you be insulted to be called a cheerleader?"

In his opinion, the first requirement for a cheer-leader was to be absolutely gorgeous. Flexibility was only a secondary requirement. He had a feeling she was both. She was certainly the first.

"Because the way you say it, it sounds as if you think cheerleaders are bubbleheaded women who share a communal brain. At the very least, they are incapable of a single creative idea."

"All that came out of one sentence, huh?" Alex marveled, impressed. "Maybe I was wrong. Maybe you *do* belong in law enforcement. And, in case you're wondering, that *was* a compliment." His eyes met hers for a moment. He felt the undercurrent of something stirring, but he couldn't put his finger on what. His sense of survival told him that it might be safer that way. "But level with me—" he began.

"Wouldn't dream of doing anything else," Valri responded.

He looked to see if she was putting him on, but she appeared serious enough.

"Yeah, well..." His voice trailed off for a moment, as if he wasn't sure if he should challenge the veracity of her statement, but then he let it go. "Then what did make you want to become a cop?" he asked, really curious now. "Was it because you wanted to 'belong'?"

"Belong?" she asked.

"Yeah. Belong," he repeated. What was so hard about the word? It seemed simple enough to him. "Everyone else in this huge family of yours is a cop, so you want to be one, too. That way you can have that in common with the others."

Valri shook her head, shooting down his theory. "Being a Cavanaugh is having something in common with the others," she reminded him. She could see that he was waiting for her to say something a little more substantial than the obvious. "*And* I thought I could do some good." That sounded hopelessly syrupy to her own ear, even though it was the truth. "Knowing that you're helping other people is just the best feeling in the whole world. Besides," she added, "I love solving puzzles. Where else can I do that and make an actual difference in people's lives but as a law enforcement agent?"

Easing his foot onto the brake as a light turned to red, Alex looked at her as if to confirm that she was indeed a flesh-and-blood female. "You can't possibly be that altruistic," he told her.

"Sure I can," she told him, not taking offense at the negativity behind his response. "And I am." With that, she changed topics. "What about your family?"

He was on his guard instantly, even though he doubted that she knew the first thing about his less than ordinary family. He'd done a good job burying their connection to him.

"What about them?" he asked guardedly.

"Are you following in anyone's footsteps?" she asked innocently.

Alex almost laughed at that. The thought that she knew about his family ceased being a concern. The innocent question told him that she didn't have a clue about what his family business was all about—or what they were really like. If he had "followed" in their footsteps, it was for an entirely different reason than the one he had suggested to her. With him it would've been a matter of being hot on one of his sibling's or his father's trail. He had been careful *not* to have that happen.

"They're not in law enforcement," he told her, trying to sound casual.

"What are they in?" she asked.

It sounded like an innocent enough question, but Alex wasn't 100 percent certain about that. She could very well be pretending to be innocent and actually feeling him out. His family's world was one of deceptions and illusions.

"Entrepreneurs," he responded. "They're entrepreneurs."

"That sounds like it could be really interesting," she commented. "Why didn't you join them?"

"Not interested," he told her. What he really wasn't interested in was staying two jumps ahead of the law. Granted there'd been a time—a very *short* period—when he'd found that exhilarating, but that was long in the past. Before he'd been labeled the official black sheep of the family.

"How many are there in your family?"

The questioning bothered him more than the silence had and he wished he had never disturbed it. At the very least, Alex didn't want to discuss his family dynamics—or anything else about them—so he turned the tables on his inquisitive partner and asked, "How many in yours?"

"Immediate or extended?"

He lifted one shoulder in a vague shrug. "Start with immediate."

"I've got six brothers and sisters—four brothers, two sisters," she explained.

That was bigger than his by threefold, he thought. "And extended?"

She laughed. "Oh God, I'm still counting. Ever since the day that Brennan saved the former chief of police from becoming that bloodthirsty serial killer's next statistic, it feels that the number just keeps growing."

"That was your brother?" he asked, surprised.

Alex was aware of the incident that she was referring to. Who lived in Aurora and *hadn't* been aware of the killing spree that had appeared to be mounted by a serial killer?

The latter had turned out to be the wife of a former police officer who had killed himself after he was fired from the police force. Blinded by grief, she decided to get even with everyone she felt had been involved in her husband's taking of his own life. But at the time, no one knew if the killer was deliberately targeting law enforcement agents or if the murders were random and the victims had just accidentally been members of the law enforcement community.

"That was Brennan all right," she confirmed. "He had to blow his cover in order to save the chief, but that's what the job's all about, right? Making judgment calls and saving people. Funny how things just seem to link up."

Where was she going with this? "What do you mean?" he asked.

"Well, if Brennan hadn't come to Uncle Andrew's rescue, none of us would have found out about this entire branch of the family that had gone missing." She grinned as she replayed her own words in her mind. "Of course, in their opinion, *we* were the ones who had gone missing all this time, but that's just splitting hairs."

"Gone missing?" he asked. She had picked up speed as she talked, and at this point her train had jumped the rails and she had completely lost him. He remembered hearing something, but since it didn't affect either him or his work directly, he'd just ignored the rest of the details as they came out.

He was beginning to realize that he shouldn't have.

His partner obligingly filled in the gaps in his

education. "It seems that my late grandfather was the former chief of police's younger brother. Their parents split up when Grandpa was about eight. His mother took him while his father had custody of Shamus—Uncle Andrew's father," she threw in to help Alex keep things straight. "She apparently took off for parts unknown with Grandpa. Time passed and Shamus lost track of the family.

"About a year ago, Shamus decided to find out what happened to his brother before any more time had gone by. Uncle Andrew did some digging—"

"And out you popped," Alex deadpanned.

If she thought he was being sarcastic, she didn't show it.

"Not exactly, but close enough," she allowed.

Valri knew when someone wanted to draw a subject to a close and she was aware of the fact that there were people who claimed to be overdosing on Cavanaughs. She, on the other hand, was thrilled to submerge herself in the family's history, learning all she could about the various members.

But it was all still very fresh and new to her, despite the fact that she had never lacked for family in any manner, shape or form in the first place. She and her siblings numbered seven and there was nearly a triple-pack of cousins, thanks to her two uncles and one aunt, so family gatherings had already become practically standing-room-only affairs. With the influx of this heretofore "hidden" branch, the current number of family members was all but overwhelming.

And Valri got a tremendous kick out of that, out of there being, according to one observer, "Cavanaughs as far as the eye can see."

"How many in your family?" she asked Alex.

He thought he'd put her off that trail by asking for details about hers. How had this come full circle back to him?

"Not nearly as many as yours," he replied, adding a silent "thank God" at the end of his sentence.

The "thank God" wasn't in reference to the fact that he found the number overwhelming, but to the fact that even though there were only three members doing something illegal at any one time, he couldn't allow his mind to even imagine more people working *his* family's business. Even three were too many in his opinion.

Yet it was the only way of life his family had ever known.

"So what is that?" Alex was asking. "Five? Ten? More?" She continued looking at him, waiting for his answer.

Damn, but she was like a pit bull, clamping down on something and refusing to let go. And he wasn't comfortable discussing his family even in the vaguest of terms.

Determined to steer her clear of this sensitive topic, Alex tried to divert her again. "Are we almost there?" he asked. After all, she was the one who professed to know the man.

Valri glanced up, focusing on the street sign they were just approaching. "Waverly," she read out loud, then pointed to the residential community's entrance. Bird of paradise plants flanked both sides like colorful, welcoming guardsmen. "You turn in at the end of the block."

He'd already assumed that, but pretended that this was news to him. "Thanks."

Valri studied his profile for a moment. His jaw, she noticed, was all but rigid.

"But you already knew that, didn't you?" she said. When he glanced in her direction, trying to look puzzled, Valri started to explain her thought process. "You're the native, right?"

"If you mean California, yes," he qualified. "But I've only lived in Aurora for the last ten years." He'd gone to college here and then just decided to stay. Aurora seemed to be as good a place as any to begin a new life. A life where he *wasn't* related to con art ists and art thieves.

"What made *you* become a cop?" she asked him, feeling that turnabout was only fair play.

Alex smiled to himself. For him, becoming a police officer had been a matter of atonement. He'd started out to make up for the rest of his family's sins. At the time, he hadn't thought that he would like the work as much as he did, or get such a feeling of satisfaction out of it. That was a bonus.

"Same as you. I wanted to do something that mattered," he told her, thinking that would be the end of it.

But after a few minutes, it seemed like only the beginning.

"Why homicide?" she asked. It seemed to her that having to deal with seeing people on the worst day of their lives would be hard on a person, certainly not something that someone would volunteer for. Yet Brody obviously had.

"I think your twenty questions are up," he told her. "And just in time," he realized. "That Wills's place?" he asked, pointing out the rather quaint-looking single-story slightly weather-beaten house to his left.

She leaned toward his side of the vehicle, looking at the house he'd pointed out. It had been a while since she'd moved in those circles, but she recognized the house.

"That's it," she told Alex.

Alex slowed his car, taking a closer look. The house appeared to be in good condition, although the front yard had been neglected. The building itself resembled a hacienda and there appeared to be a fresh coat of light gray paint on the stucco.

"Pretty nice," Alex commented. "Wills must be doing well."

She debated letting him think that, but there was no point in it. "It's his mother's house. She left it to him in her will so he wouldn't wind up living in a cardboard box under some bridge after she was gone."

He took another long look at the residence. Closer examination had him picking up on the chipped paint at the corners, and there appeared to be a couple of tiles missing from the roof.

"You're telling me that he's *not* doing so well, then."

"What I'm saying is that Wills had a tendency to come in third or fourth in the competitions that did have a payoff. He lives for the game and the glory." Her mouth curved in an ironic smile. "Money is something that he borrows, not earns."

That sounded like a philosophy that was dog-eared for extermination. "That could get old fast," Alex commented. "Didn't he run out of 'friends' to tap?"

"He did," she told him. "That's why he liked hanging around Rogers. He got the spotlight that he craved by being in Rogers's sphere and Rogers liked being the big man and tossing Wills a scrap or two, something he never did quietly."

"Meaning?" Alex asked, wanting to have everything as clear as possible before going in.

He pulled up in the driveway.

"Meaning that Rogers would make a big deal out

of whatever so-called good deed he did so that everyone knew that he was being 'magnanimous' and keeping Wills afloat."

Well, that certainly went along with what he was thinking. "Not much of a stretch envisioning Wills killing Rogers for revenge and whatever pocket money the other had."

But Valri wasn't buying it. She shook her head. "Don't think so. Wills loved being in Rogers's spotlight. I think he hoped some of Rogers's skills, as well as his luck, would rub off on him. But I could be wrong," she allowed. This was just another theory she was formulating.

"Well, no time like the present to find out."

Alex pressed the doorbell, but heard nothing in return. He tried again with the same results. Doubling up his fist, he pounded on the door.

"Randolph Wills, this is the Aurora Police Department. Open up!"

When there was still no response, Valri nudged him out of the way and knocked rather than pounded on the door. "Hey, Randy," she called out through the door, "it's Wren295. I've got to talk to you about The King."

Alex stared at her as if she had suddenly slipped through the rabbit hole right before his eyes. "What the hell are you talking about?"

Before she had a chance to answer him, the front door opened.

Chapter 5

Randolph Wills was a rather nondescript thin man anyone could have passed on the street without noticing at all. Everything about the thirty-ish gamer was painfully average—except for his eyes. A deep brown and constantly alert, his eyes moved around with the speed of two balls in play in a pinball machine. Wills took in all of his surroundings, processing everything, retaining it for future use.

As he kept the door only partially open, his eyes passed over the woman he knew by her former gamer handle and then slid over the man standing next to her. A frown twisted his thin lips.

"You're not alone," he accused. The next moment, he started to swing his front door closed again.

He wasn't fast enough. Valri had anticipated his reaction and had her foot positioned so that it acted like a doorstop.

"He's a friend," she told the gamer.

"He ain't my friend," Wills retorted.

While he eagerly mingled with everyone at video game conventions, anyone outside that world was held suspect. Verging on being upset, Wills attempted to kick Valri's foot out of the way.

At this point, Alex blocked the door with his shoulder, preventing the far weaker gamer from budging it. "We'll make 'nice' later," Alex told the gamer. "Right now, we've got some questions to ask you about Hunter Rogers."

At the mention of the slain gamer, Wills's expression changed. He looked furtively from the woman he knew to the man he didn't. Bravado gave way to nerves.

His breathing grew audible as he asked, "He send you here?"

Valri exchanged glances with her partner. "Why would he send us?" she asked Wills gently.

"'Cause he said he wanted—" Wills stopped abruptly, and while the fear he had displayed didn't entirely vanish, it did lessen. A note of suspicion entered the man's demeanor. "If he didn't send you, why are you here?" he asked.

"We need to ask you a few questions, Randy."

She nodded toward the darkened living room behind him. "May we come in?"

Wills shrugged, his almost pointy shoulders rising and then falling in a vague, careless movement. "Yeah, I guess so. You don't touch anything," he warned Alex gruffly, then went on to tell Valri, "You can if you want to. I've got a spare controller if you want to join in. It's a beauty. Gold," he said almost reverently about the gaming device.

Pushing the front door open all the way, Wills led the pair into his living room.

The entire front of the house had been converted to an open game pit with a giant screen displaying the current game—one involving zombie troops fighting a battalion of marines for control of Earth. The light coming from the monitor was the only illumination in the room.

The aura was rather gloomy, Alex thought. He was surprised to hear his new partner comment to the other man, "Nice. But we're not here to play."

Wills had already dropped onto the giant sofa facing the monitor. His entire being focused on the screen, he picked up his controller. As if it were a talisman, holding it made the gamer sit up a little straighter, appear a little more confident.

"I think better after a game. Helps clear my head. You play me—and win—" he smirked as he said the word, clearly thinking that was an impossibility "—and I'll answer anything you want."

Valri regarded the gamer, weighing his offer against standard procedure. "Truthfully? I have your word?"

"You've got my word," Wills answered cavalierly.

"Okay," Valri agreed. "You're on." Sitting down on the sofa, Valri picked up the controller Wills had gushed about.

This was not the way he conducted interviews, Alex thought impatiently. Served him right for agreeing to being partnered with this rookie.

"Cavanaugh," he began, a clear warning note in his voice.

She flashed him a wide smile. "This'll just take a few minutes, Brody," she promised.

"Ha! You wish," Wills crowed as one of his characters decimated one of hers.

"We can haul him into the precinct for questioning," Alex told her. "There's no need to descend to his level and feed his ego first."

"You're a cop?" Wills asked accusingly, his voice rising several octaves.

"Everybody has to be something," Valri told the gamer, her eyes never wavering from the screen. A second later, her avatar had managed to blow up two members of Wills's undead army.

Clearly unnerved at the loss he hadn't foreseen, Wills became sloppier as his need to win trumped his skills. Choking when it was crucial not to, Wills proved to be an easy opponent.

The game was over in less than fifteen minutes with Valri coming out the winner.

"It's not fair," Wills pouted darkly. "You got into my head and messed with it."

Setting the controller down on the scarred and dirt-encrusted coffee table in front of her, Valri turned toward the gamer and smiled.

"Just part of the game, Randy. I did my part," she said, referring to her win. "Now it's time for you to live up to yours."

He glared at her, nursing his wounds. "What do you want to know?" he asked grudgingly.

Having held his peace for far longer than he cared to, Alex jumped in with the first question. "For starters, when did you last see Hunter Rogers?"

Wills looked toward the woman who had beaten him. When she nodded that he should consider her partner's question as part of the deal, Wills asked him, "You mean The King?"

Alex in turn looked at Valri, as well. The reference meant nothing to him, but she had used it to gain access into the house, so he was rather unsure of his answer. "Do I?" he asked.

Valri nodded. "You do. When did you last see The King?" she repeated, her eyes pinning Wills down.

Another hapless shrug had Wills's bony shoulders moving up and down almost spasmodically. "I can't remember."

Valri didn't believe him. She looked at the gamer closely. When she spoke, she sounded as if she was disappointed in him.

"Randy, you promised me you'd tell the truth. You might not remember to pay your bills on time, but I'm betting that you remember seeing Rogers. I bet that you could probably cite *every* time you spoke to The King, not to mention every word he ever said to you."

In her opinion, the gamer was the ultimate obsessive fan, bordering on being considered a stalker in the making.

Wills took it as a compliment and preened in response.

"Maybe," he allowed loftily. "What's he saying?" Wills asked, no doubt still a little leery as to why his idol had sent two law enforcement agents to his home. "Is he complaining 'cause I got on his case?" Not waiting for an answer, Wills drew himself up importantly. "I did it for his own good. I told The King not to have anything to do with it. That's when he threw me out. Didn't want to hear it."

"To do with what?" Alex pressed, annoyed that the gamer was avoiding being pinned down.

Wills's head all but swiveled as he looked from the detective to the woman. "What those people wanted him to do. But The King said the money was too good to pass up. I told him he was crazy." Wills frowned as he relived the incident. "And *that's* when he actually threw me out." The gamer sighed dramatically. "What's he saying now?" Wills asked again, his eyes shifting back and forth like a table tennis ball during a well-matched tournament.

"Not much of anything," Alex answered flippantly, then asked what was really on his mind. "What people are you referring to?"

But Wills's attention had gravitated to something the detective had said, refusing to go forward.

"What's he talking about?" the gamer asked Valri, jerking his thumb back at the detective who had come in with her. "What does he mean by saying 'not much of anything'? Is The King sick? Did that lowlife give him something to make him sick?" His voice went up an octave, sounding almost shrill as his panic mounted, growing to near unmanageable proportions.

Valri glanced at her partner to see if he had any objections, but if he did, he wasn't mentioning them. The next moment, she braced herself for more drama as she said, "Randy, I'm afraid he's not sick, he's dead."

Randy stared at her, openmouthed and clearly flirting with shock. "No, he's not," he firmly insisted. "He's just doing this to get even with me for bugging him. Right? Right?" he asked a bit more sharply. At this point, the gamer was pleading. "Tell me he's just trying to get even with me, Wren. *Please.*"

The one thing she believed in above all else was telling the truth.

"I can't do that, Randy," she said kindly. "It'd be a lie. Someone shot Hunter Rogers."

At this point, Wills's emotional gauge was waffling between anger and despair.

"I knew it, I knew it, I knew it. I told him they were dangerous, that he was getting in over his head. But all he saw were those damn dollar signs dancing in front of his eyes. Now look where that got him," he declared, then added in disgust, "Dead."

"What people?" Valri asked. "What did they want him to do?"

"They wanted him to come up with some kind of new code to use for a hacking job," Wills said before he could think better of it. He looked flustered about the information, sparse though it was, that he had just allowed to be said.

"What *kind* of a hacking job?" Alex asked. "Did you see any of them, hear any of their names?" he pressed, aware that the chances of that were slim to none. But he had to ask.

For just a split second, it looked as if the gamer was about to answer Alex's questions. But then Wills clamped his mouth.

When he spoke again, it was to tell them that he wasn't about to say another word—and why.

"If these people killed The King," he said mournfully, tearing up as he spoke about his dead idol, "then they'll be sure to kill me if I say another word."

"Randy, you know me. You know I won't let that happen to you," Valri promised.

"How?" Wills asked.

"We'll put you in protective custody," Alex told the shorter man.

"Protective custody," Wills echoed disdainfully before shaking his head. "Not good enough," he said, dismissing the offer. "I want that witness thing. You know what I'm talking about. I get set up somewhere else with a new name, better lifestyle…"

"Witness protection program?" Alex guessed.

He was about to say that it would be a different lifestyle, not necessarily an upgrade from the one he had. Alex doubted that the slight man before him would be happy doing anything except living in front of a monitor, looking at a depiction of some fantasy world or other.

Wills leaped on the term. "Yeah, that's the one. I want that. And I want something in writing that says you're not going to find a sneaky way to throw me into jail. That's another thing I want," he announced as if this idea had just now occurred to him. "I want immunization."

"You mean immunity," Valri corrected gently.

"Whatever," the gamer said.

Alex frowned at his partner. She was treating this parasite with kid gloves. He supposed he should have been glad she was along. Left on his own, he would have backed the gamer into a corner, used a couple of well-placed verbal threats about what might befall someone who withheld information that would impede a homicide investigation and allowed the man's imagination to run away with him.

Still, he was willing to give her way a little while longer before he ironed the wrinkles out of Wills's shirt—with him in it.

"Okay, you've got it," Alex told him. "Now talk."

"Not so fast." The gamer held up his hand. "I wasn't born yesterday. I get to see this in writing, signed by whoever makes the deals in your department, *then* I'll tell you what you want to know. Not before," he added stubbornly, folding his arms before him and projecting an air of a man who knew he had something of importance to trade.

Alex wasn't saying a word, but she could guess that what was going through her new partner's mind was not a docile agreement to the terms. Brody did not strike her as a man who could be dictated to.

"Okay, we can make that happen," Valri told the gamer. "Why don't you come with us while I get that statement for you from the DA's office?"

But Wills shook his head. "Uh-uh. I'm not going anywhere. I leave here, I lose home-field advantage," he told her. "I know how this works. You bring me back my deal and I'll sing like a canary."

Alex curbed the very strong desire to pick up the slight man and just bodily carry him to his vehicle.

"We can make that happen," Valri repeated. Turning toward her partner, she said, "Let's go." As she reached the front door, she looked over her shoulder at Wills and told him, "We'll be back soon."

Alex waited until they were on the other side of the front door before saying another word. "Can I ask *how* we're going to make that happen so fast?" the detective asked.

Valri was relieved to have an answer for him. "The chief of Ds' daughter, Janelle, is an ADA."

"Of course she is," Alex muttered.

He was aware of the fact that one of the chief's brothers, Sean, was the head of the day shift in the crime scene investigation unit. He also knew that the former chief of police had been the eldest of the Cavanaughs, Andrew.

"Tell me," he asked as they walked to the driveway, where his vehicle was parked, "is there a Cavanaugh for everything?"

Rather than take offense at the slightly sarcastic edge in his voice, Valri laughed and said, "That depends on what you mean by 'everything.'"

He was not about to get into a debate over semantics. As far as he was concerned, she'd just given him his answer.

"I thought so," he responded with a sigh. Alex glanced over his shoulder toward the house just before he got into the driver's seat. "Still think we should just haul him in."

"We do and he'll just clam up and refuse to talk," she pointed out. Getting in, Valri buckled up and waited for Brody to start the car.

Alex put the key into the ignition. "Yeah, until I raise my voice, then he'll trip over his own tongue, talking so fast he'll practically choke on his words."

She had a slightly different take on that. She knew that gamers had an image of being these nerd-like, almost subterranean creatures who never came up for daylight. Hackers, however, had a completely different image. They were the dangerous ones.

"Not if he's more afraid of these 'people,' whoever they are, than he is of a forceful detective who shouts, but when the chips are down, can't shoot him. You can't hurt him. They can."

Alex was still unconvinced. "I think that giving that guy a wedgie would have him cringing in fear and spilling the beans."

Valri laughed. "My way's more peaceful," she told him.

Alex pretended to evaluate her response. "What fun is that?" he countered.

"You are pulling my leg, aren't you?" She was only half kidding when she asked.

In his company for a limited time, Valri was still trying to figure the man out. She couldn't tell when he was joking, and when he was serious. She did know, however, that he was less patient than she was, but then, his family didn't number in the legions. That sort of thing, especially when you're one of the youngest members, teaches a great deal of patience.

"Maybe yes, maybe no," Alex answered. "Tell me, just how well do you know this Cavanaugh ADA?"

Valri didn't try to sugarcoat it. "I've met her a couple of times at the family parties. But more important than that, she's a Cavanaugh and unless I'm completely wrong about this, and I'm not," she told him with a degree of certainty he found impressive, "she wouldn't undermine an investigation, especially a homicide investigation, unless it is completely baseless, and this isn't. Randy is *dying* to talk about the people the victim was doing business with."

"How can you be so sure?" Alex challenged.

"Because in his eyes, this makes him important by proxy. Rogers had made a name for himself in some circles. Randy's name is mud in *any* circle. I guarantee that nobody even knows who he is—other than the gamer who was The King's shadow—so Randy's trying to get a little of Rogers's spotlight to rub off on him. The only way he can do that now is to say he knows who The King's killer is—or are," she amended in case there was more than one person involved in the actual murder.

"Doesn't he know that it's guilt by association, not glitter by association?" Alex asked.

If the gamer knew who killed Rogers and wasn't stepping forward, then he was guilty of impeding an investigation—and that carried a penalty with it.

Valri read between the lines and understood what her partner was referring to. "Some people grab what they can get."

He supposed that she was right.

On the main thoroughfare through Aurora, he was driving back to the precinct out of habit. But Cavanaugh had said she wanted to get that written statement from the ADA and the ADA was not located in the same building as the police department.

Glancing to his right, he said to his temporary partner, "So we're going...?"

"Straight to the ADA's office." Her mouth curved slightly as a piece of an old cartoon movie line suddenly played itself in her head. "'Second star to the right, straight out 'til morning,'" she added.

"The ADA doubles as Peter Pan in her spare time?" Alex questioned, raising an eyebrow.

Just exactly who was this person the chief had shackled him to, temporarily or not? She certainly didn't come across like any cop he'd ever known.

"No." Valri laughed, surprised that he even got the reference. "Sorry, I couldn't resist. I was trying to ease your tension."

He shot her a look. "And what makes you think I'm tense?"

She'd seen less rigid posture on a graduating West Point cadet. But rather than point that out, Valri merely said, "Just a hunch. I'm tense so I figured you had to be."

"Well, you figured wrong," he informed her. He wasn't tense, he was annoyed—big-time—and there was nothing she could do to change that.

Except to stay put in the squad room the next time he went out in the field.

Chapter 6

ADA Janelle Cavanaugh Boone came very close to colliding with her younger cousin as Valri was about to cross the threshold to her office moving at what seemed like top speed.

Swallowing a startled cry, Janelle managed to catch herself just in time.

"I got your request," Janelle said to her cousin, referring to Valri's cell phone call that had gone to voice mail. "I've got no problem with it, but can it wait until morning?"

Her arms were filled with two files that were overflowing with papers, and a briefcase attached to a strap was hanging off her shoulder right next to her actual shoulder bag. All in all, the chief of detectives' only daughter looked like the poster child for harried businesswomen everywhere.

Valri flashed her an apologetic yet amazingly hopeful smile.

"It really can't. The witness is extremely skittish and we're afraid he might just skip town if we can't come back to him with this deal in writing."

She had mentioned a few of the particulars, summarizing the case, when she'd called and left her message on Janelle's voice mail.

Valri looked hopefully at her cousin.

Juggling her files, Janelle seemed to waver, but this matter was important, as well.

"This witness of yours, is he reliable?"

Valri almost said that she "thought" so, then decided that a more positive response was necessary. "Yes, in my opinion, he is."

Janelle sighed.

"Come in," she told the duo, motioning them into her office with her head.

Walking in ahead of them, she emptied her arms, dropping the files, her briefcase and her bag onto her desk. A thud confirmed the deposit.

Janelle opened a drawer and after a minimum of searching, she located a form. Signing it with a flourish, she held out the paper to her cousin.

"I'm trusting you to fill in the particulars." Just

before she let Valri take the form, she asked, "You're sure this won't come back and bite me?"

Valri held up her right hand as if she were taking an oath. "I give you my word."

"Good enough for me," Janelle pronounced.

Gathering up the things she had just set on her desk, she glanced over at Alex. Other than nodding at her, he hadn't said a word.

"Your partner?" she asked Valri.

"Temporarily," Alex emphasized, saying the word half a beat ahead of the ADA's cousin.

"Do you have a name, 'temporary partner'?" Janelle asked, seemingly amused by the thinly veiled protest.

"Detective Alex Brody," he told her.

"Look after my cousin, Detective Alex Brody. The family just found her," she told the man. "We definitely don't want to lose her so quickly. We've barely gotten acquainted."

Alex inclined his head. "I'll do my best, ma'am."

Janelle winced. With a toss of her head, she appeared to dismiss the offense. The smile she offered Brody was warm, confident and utterly reassuring.

"I'm sure you will, Detective. I'm sure you will." Her arms tightening around the files she'd just picked up, she made a parting comment to Valri. "Let me know how this all turns out."

"Absolutely," Valri promised. "And thank you," she called after her cousin, whose pace had picked up. The sound of her high heels clicked rhythmically as she made her way down the hall.

"We all have to do our part," she told Valri.

Janelle was gone before Valri could respond. Turning to Alex, she glanced over the paper that Janelle had just signed, then held it out for Alex to look over, as well. "Looks like we've got our bait, Brody. Let's go."

"Thanks for letting me tag along," he responded wryly. Considering the exchange between Cavanaugh and her cousin, in his opinion a cardboard figure could have taken his place.

Valri stopped just short of the elevator and turned to face him. She hadn't meant to make him feel belittled.

"Sorry," she apologized. "I have a tendency to get carried away and take over."

"Really?" Brody said sarcastically. "I hadn't noticed."

Okay, she'd obviously hurt his ego, but that certainly hadn't been her intent. Her apology *should* have leveled the playing field.

"I apologized," she pointed out needlessly. "What more would you like me to do?"

Now *that* was a loaded line, he couldn't help thinking.

"Oh, so many things I don't even know where to begin, Cavanaugh. But for now, let's just go back and get that posturing little gamer out of his cave and into protective custody. I'll call the marshal's department to get the ball rolling so that he'll have his new identity all set up by the end of tomorrow."

Valri nodded her agreement. "I'm not going to be able to relax until we get Randy out of there and into a hotel room."

Well, at least they agreed on some things, Alex thought. "That makes two of us."

When they arrived at Randy Wills's house twenty minutes later, Alex parked his car in the driveway just the way he did the first time. And, just like the first time, there were no actual lights coming from the house, only the hint of a glow from the TV monitor that dominated the gaming pit, otherwise once known as the living room.

Getting out quickly, Alex reached the front door first. When he began to knock, the door moved beneath his knuckles.

Frowning, he slowly tried the doorknob and found that the door wasn't locked.

"This can't be good," Valri murmured to herself, then out loud she looked toward her partner and commented, "I don't think I like this."

"Looks like that makes two of us again," Alex said. Drawing his weapon, he slowly eased the door open with his free hand.

Valri had her own gun out as she entered half a step behind her partner.

At first glance, everything looked the way it had

when they had previously entered the house. The lights were off, and the TV monitor that took up such a large part of the room was running the same video game that had been on earlier.

And Wills was sitting on the sofa, apparently so consumed with the action on the monitor that he wasn't aware of anything else. There didn't appear to be anyone else in the house.

"We've got your deal, Wills," Alex called out. "Right here on this paper from the ADA. All nice and legal. All you have to do is sign it and you can start your new life."

The gamer didn't answer him or even acknowledge his presence.

And there was something else he wasn't doing, Valri noticed. Rather than say anything, she caught her partner by the arm. When Brody looked at her quizzically, she pointed to the controller in the gamer's hand.

"His hands aren't moving," she said in a quiet voice, dropping her own hand from Brody's arm. "He's not playing."

Brody stalked around the sofa so he could get a frontal view of the gamer. He lightly put his hand on the gamer's shoulder. The man instantly slumped over in the opposite direction.

"He's dead," Valri pronounced.

Alex put two fingers to the gamer's neck area,

looking for any sign of a pulse. There was nothing, not even a hint of life struggling to continue.

"Looks that way to me," Alex agreed. He scanned the immediate area. "There's no sign of a struggle."

"Or a break-in," Valri concurred. "He knew his killer."

"Either that, or the killer had a spare key," Alex suggested.

Valri shook her head. "I don't think so. If the killer had let himself in, he would have used that key to lock up when he left."

"Maybe he's not a neat freak," Alex countered.

"It has nothing to do with being neat," she told him. "He'd lock the door behind him to add to the air of mystery, put another bump in the road. No, I think Randy let whoever wound up killing him in. Which means that it was—"

"Another gamer," Alex concluded. "Our boy here doesn't strike me as a well-rounded person with his share of friends," he guessed. "He'd only know other gamers and geek types."

"I'll pretend you didn't say that," she told him.

"Present company excluded," he said, inclining his head toward her. "Besides, you're not a gamer, you're a cop, remember?"

She gazed down at the face of the man who had been alive just a short while ago. "I remember," she replied grimly.

Alex took a handkerchief out of his back pocket

and used it to keep from touching the light switch on the wall as he flipped it on. Despite the illumination that flooded the room, the pervading aura of gloom continued.

The video game was partially at fault for that. Alex rectified that next by turning off the set.

With the added light, Alex could see things more clearly. Circling the victim, he came up behind the gamer again and was able to make out what he hadn't seen the first time.

"He was shot from behind."

"Execution style," Valri confirmed.

"Think the killer was trying to make some sort of a statement with that?" Alex asked.

"Yes—that he was acting out some secret agent/ spy fantasy. I did a quick background check on Randy before we came to talk to him the first time—"

"A background check?" Alex echoed. "I thought you said you knew him."

"I did, but just in a passing sense. I didn't want us to have any surprises."

Alex shook his head. "Well, that didn't exactly work out well, did it?"

She looked down at the gamer, thinking what a terrible waste it was to have life snatched away at such a young age. "No, I guess not."

"Call this in," Alex told her. "We're going to need forensics to go over this place with a fine-tooth comb. Who knows, the killer might not have been as careful as he thought he was."

Valri took out her cell phone to do as he'd suggested. "What are you going to be doing while I'm calling?" she asked.

"I'm going to make sure that our killer isn't by some chance hiding in any of the closets."

"He's not," she told him as she started to place her call.

Walking to the rear of the house, Alex stopped. "What makes you so sure?" he asked.

"No car in the driveway, no car parked at the curb or nearby," she pointed out.

"Maybe our killer is a public transportation kind of guy," Alex countered.

The expression on her face was highly skeptical. "The man just offed another man. He'd be much too wired, much too high on adrenaline, to calmly ride a bus back to wherever he came from."

"You don't mind if I just satisfy my own curiosity and check, do you?" he asked sarcastically.

"Not in the slightest," she assured him.

And then he watched her become alert. Obviously someone had just picked up on the other end of the call.

"Yes," he heard his partner saying, then giving her shield number to identify herself. "We need someone from the coroner's office to come pick up a body. Yes, a *human* body," she stressed. Pressing the mute button on her cell, she looked in Brody's direction. "What kind of calls go into the coroner's office?" she asked in wonder.

Alex laughed. "You'd be surprised," he told her. "They rake in more prank calls than the other departments combined. Gallows humor, I think it's called."

But he could see that the lively blonde was no longer listening to him. Her attention was exclusively focused on the voice coming from her cell phone.

There was no one else in the 1,400-square-foot house. He'd gone into every closet, looked under every bed, searched every inch of space. Other than rumpled sheets on a double bed in what he assumed was the master bedroom, there was not even any indication that anyone had been in the rooms, other than the gaming pit.

"Satisfied?" Valri asked him when he came back to the scene of the crime.

He wasn't a person who ignored the obvious— even when he would have liked to. "You were right, there wasn't anyone there."

"But there will be soon," she said as she heard the distant wail of sirens in the background—growing louder as they came closer.

Processing the crime scene took more than two hours for the CSI team. Alex realized that his presence on the site, as well as Cavanaugh's, wasn't necessary, but he was anxious to see if the investigators could come up with something he could physically use when he went in search of his quarry the next day.

He decided to pack it in when nothing useful seemed to turn up. By then, their day was supposed to have ended a couple of hours ago.

When they got back to the precinct parking lot, Alex dropped her off by her car, said "good night," and was about to drive off when Valri called out, "See you in the morning."

See you in the morning.

It was the kind of sentence that inherently spawned the juvenile comeback "Not if I see you first."

He refrained from saying it, but his thoughts were his own.

Any way he emphasized it, those simple words changed his destination from home to the hospital. There was someone he needed to touch base with.

Tonight.

Lying in the hospital bed, his eyes all but glazed over out of boredom, Jake Montgomery listlessly looked over toward the door when he heard it opening. A tall hulk of a man who looked completely out of place in a hospital bed, he instantly brightened when he saw who was walking into his room.

"Hey, Brody," he cried, grinning. "Come to see if I was a corpse yet?"

Alex dropped into the orange plastic chair beside his partner's bed. "No, I came to see if you were tired of faking it and ready to come back to work."

"Faking it?" Montgomery echoed indignantly. "You try getting run over by a tricked-out Jeep SUV and see how good *you* feel."

"Yeah, yeah, yeah," Alex said, waving a dismissive hand at his partner's words of protest. "All I know is that you'd do anything to get some time off with pay, even pull a fool stunt like that to get out of doing any of your paperwork. Well, FYI, those reports are piling up, and I don't care if they block out the sun, I'm not cleaning those files up. That's your mess."

Shifting in his chair, Alex leaned in closer to Montgomery. "Seriously, buddy, you've got to concentrate on getting well and out of this bed. I need you back on the job, like yesterday."

They'd been partners for three years now and this was the most serious he'd ever been with his partner. It obviously caught Montgomery off guard. "Since when?" Montgomery asked.

"Since the chief of Ds made me chief babysitter to his niece—or grandniece, or whatever she's supposed to be called, although between you and me, 'pain in the butt' is more apt a description for the likes of her. The woman is making me crazy."

Montgomery stared at him, surprise etched all over his wide, hangdog face. "You've got a new partner?" he asked.

Alex was rather surprised that Montgomery hadn't heard yet. Were they keeping his partner in the dark for a reason? he wondered. Or was there some other reason not to keep Montgomery up on the latest news?

He was quick to do damage control in case Montgomery found the news upsetting. "It's just temporary. You know, like being sent to purgatory is just temporary, until you're deemed worthy and pure enough to enter heaven. As far as I'm concerned, I'm good to go anytime now. I've got the scars to prove it."

Flashing the bedridden man an encouraging grin, Alex rose from the chair. "I'd better let you get your rest. The faster you heal, the faster you come back to the squad room," he said cheerfully, savoring the image of that for a moment. "I'll even listen to your corny jokes—at least in the beginning," he amended in the interest of being honest.

"Brody, about that," Montgomery began hesitantly, stopping Alex in his tracks as surely as if he had put a nail gun to good use and nailed down the soles of his partner's shoes.

"What about it?" Alex asked, his throat suddenly growing exceedingly dry. A premonition undulated through him. He wasn't all that certain he wanted to hear what was coming next. But he also knew that he didn't exactly have a choice.

He hated being blindsided.

"Annie wants me to take a desk job in the department when I get off medical leave," Montgomery began, mentioning his wife of twenty-one years. "She's got this crazy notion that I've used up my supply of good luck and that there's still a bullet with my name on it out there, waiting to find me.

"If I'm out in the field, sooner or later, it *will* find me," Montgomery guaranteed. "Nothing personal, Brody. You've been a great partner and I wouldn't even be here now if it weren't for you, I know that. You saved my life. But Annie made it clear—fieldwork or her, I have to choose. I can't have both and I kinda gotten used to having her around. At my age, where am I going to find someone who'll put up with me? I'm not exactly George Clooney, you know."

Alex felt as if he'd just slipped into one of those old Warner Brothers cartoons and the coyote was holding up a safe, waiting to drop it on the unsuspecting roadrunner. He knew that the safe should somehow wind up dropping on the coyote, but it didn't. The rope had snapped and the safe was heading straight for the roadrunner.

And in an odd twist, it looked as if *he* was the roadrunner.

Chapter 7

"You understand, don't you, Brody?" Montgomery asked him uneasily after a couple of minutes had passed and he still hadn't said anything.

There was no point in snapping at his partner, Alex thought, or in telling him to "man up." Thanks to practically being mowed down by the suspect's Jeep SUV, Montgomery had come face-to-face with his own mortality and it had done a number on the man, he got that. He was even sympathetic toward what his partner was going through.

Besides, just because Montgomery was bailing on him didn't automatically mean that the hot little number that the chief had assigned to him was going to wind up being his *permanent* partner. Their teaming up was labeled *temporary* right from the start and he intended to hold the chief of Ds and the chirpy little blonde to that with every fiber of his being.

Easy on the eyes though she was, he wasn't ready to be paired up with either a rookie or an almighty Cavanaugh—certainly not someone who was *both*. He preferred partners who didn't come with a pedigree and who could carry their own load *by themselves*. Someone who had gotten to where he or she was through pure merit, not nepotism.

"Sure I understand, Montgomery. A good woman versus possibly being on the receiving end of a game-ending bullet. That's a no-brainer from where I'm standing. You've got to keep your wife happy, right?" Alex forced a grin to his lips. He'd gotten good at that. Faking it while keeping his real feelings totally under wraps. "After all, she's the one you come home to every night."

Banged up though he still was, Montgomery brightened visibly. "Thanks, partner. That's a real load off my mind. Speaking of coming home at night, soon as I'm up and about, you're coming over for dinner, you hear? Bring your current squeeze of the moment, too," his about-to-be-former partner added.

"Yeah, sure." Alex rose from the thickly upholstered chair. "Well, I'd better let you get your rest.

They toss you out of these places as fast as they can so you might as well be up to it."

"I am kind of tired," Montgomery admitted. Using the remote control that was fastened to his side railing, he pressed the down button and the upper portion of his mattress slowly lowered until it was almost flat. "See you when I blow this joint," he promised.

"See you," Alex echoed.

His partner was asleep before he reached the door.

Ex-partner, Alex amended. He frowned as he walked down the corridor. He was going to have to get used to thinking of Montgomery in the past tense.

And thinking of Cavanaugh *only* in the present tense, he added tersely.

He entertained the idea of hitting Malone's on his way home, then decided against it. The way he felt right now, it was going to take more than just one beer to unclench his insides. He didn't feel like leaving his car in the bar's parking lot and calling a cab to drive him home.

Stopping at the first grocery store he came to, Alex bought a bottle of Southern Comfort liqueur and hoped it would live up to its name.

Her eyes felt as if someone had deliberately glued them shut, and there was this quick, sharp pain in her neck when she moved her head a little to the right.

She knew better than to attempt to stretch. Her muscles would all cramp up.

That was the price she paid for falling asleep at her desk, Valri thought ruefully, annoyed with herself. She really hadn't meant to doze off at her workstation, and she certainly hadn't intended to spend the night in the squad room.

The problem was she had kept giving herself "just a few more minutes" as she wrestled with the knotty problem of attempting to resurrect the smashed laptop. She kept moving forward by fractions of an inch.

Whoever had taken the sledgehammer to the laptop had obviously thought that was enough to kill any and all data on the hard drive. Overconfidence caused whoever had done it not to take the extra precaution of wiping the hard drive clean, as well.

That was where the person made a mistake, Valri thought with a whisper of a smile curving her mouth.

The data might no longer be visible, but it was still there, a phantom shadow shimmering somewhere out in space, waiting to be restored. It was up to her to coax it back by finding just the right combination of keys, the right subprogram.

That required an infinite amount of patience and dexterity.

Lucky for her she had both.

Because as it happened, "a few more minutes" wound up stretching out into an hour and then two. After that, she lost track and gave up the idea of remaining for only "a few more minutes." At that point, she knew she was there for the duration.

A small battalion of squashed paper cups that had once each contained some pretty bad black coffee from the vending machine had grown into an untidy pyramid in her wastebasket.

The infusion of the coffee had helped a little, keeping her awake far longer than she was accustomed to, but eventually, the rather foul-tasting black ooze had ceased working its minimal magic and she had given in to mental and physical exhaustion. She promised herself a break that shared the same dubious parameters she'd given herself about unlocking the secrets of the laptop: just a few minutes.

By the way her neck and eyelids felt and the manner the rest of her body complained—her position against her desk had been just shy of the one assumed by penitent early Christian martyrs—her "time-out" had been a period far longer than "just a few minutes."

Forcing herself to sit up as straight as she could, Valri rotated her neck, first in one direction, then in the opposite one. She was trying her best to loosen the muscles up.

By the sharp, quick stabbing pains that were registering, it really wasn't working.

What she needed was a good massage, but there was no way she was going to be able to fit that into her day's routine. This would just have to work itself out on its own.

"Does it come off when you do that?"

Thinking herself almost alone on this side of the squad room, the unexpected question coming from directly behind her made her jump. Valri clutched her armrests and turned in her seat.

Brody.

She blinked, clearing away the partial blur that had descended over her eyes, and focused on his face.

Was it her imagination, or did *he* look somewhat *blurry*—for lack of a better term? This wasn't the somewhat cocky, bright-eyed detective she'd made the rounds with yesterday.

What had happened?

"You look as bad as I feel," she told Brody.

"Thanks," Alex bit off, wearily dropping into his chair. His head was killing him despite the two ibuprofen he'd popped into his mouth as he walked out the door. Pills that promised to vanquish his headache within twenty minutes, if not sooner.

Obviously his headache operated by different rules and most decidedly on a different timetable.

"You're in early," he commented. Then as he

brought his container of coffee up to his mouth, his eyes narrowed and he looked at her for the first time. "Or you stayed late, as the case may be." Taking a deep drink, he assessed the situation, his eyes never shifting away from her. "You never went home, did you? I recognize your clothes," he told her. "You were wearing the exact same thing yesterday."

That wasn't very hard to figure out, she thought, annoyed at what she took to be his superior tone. "Very good, Brody. You get a gold star for being so observant—almost like a detective. You'd better hang on to that little skill. It just might parlay itself into a career for you someday. How are you at reading palms?" she asked innocently, holding up her right hand for him to look at.

"Your lifeline goes on forever," he observed, impressed.

Surprised to hear his assessment, Valri pulled her hand back and looked down on it. He'd gotten it wrong.

"That's not my lifeline. That's a scar that feeds into my lifeline," she told him. "I got that one when I was a kid."

"Bending steel with your bare hands at a young age, were you?" Alex asked.

She shook her head, overlooking what someone else might have taken as blatant sarcasm. "Fighting with one of my brothers. I don't remember which one at the moment." Since he was asking questions, she had one of her own. "Why do you look like something the cat rejected bringing in?" she asked.

"Long story." He'd discovered that Southern Comfort liqueur went down way too easy and took its sweet time in numbing his mind.

Valri cocked her head, obviously still waiting for something more. "Is there a woman in it?" she asked, the question coming out of left field as far as he was concerned.

Alex stared at her. Did she know? "What?"

"Were you trying to drown your sorrows last night because of a woman?" Valri asked.

He laughed shortly, thinking it ironic that the cause for his solitary bender would phrase her question just that way.

"In a manner of speaking, yes," he answered. "Now, if we can get out of my private life and back into the reason that we both draw paychecks from the police department—"

"Fine by me," she said, raising her hands from the laptop's keyboard as if she was in the process of surrendering.

Nodding at the laptop, he knew that Cavanaugh was waiting for him to ask, so he obliged her. "Did you find anything?"

She could tell by the tone of Brody's voice that the hungover detective sincerely doubted she had made any headway. Apparently he was just asking the question to humor her.

She *really* wished she had been more success-ful than she had been, but at least she had gotten her toe wet. And she wasn't about to stop until she had a lot more.

"The data is pretty mangled," she began.

"Yeah, that's what I figured," Alex commented dismissively.

He took a long pull from his coffee. Rather than settle for his caffeine hit via what was in the vend-ing machine, or the stuff brewing in the break area, he'd brought his coffee straight from home. There was currently enough caffeine in his cup to raise a herd of dead elephants. He was counting on it to kick-start his brain.

"But I did manage to get a few bits and pieces of his email correspondences," Valri continued, doing her best not to crow about it—even though she dearly wanted to.

Alex stopped drinking his coffee. "You actually *got* something?" he questioned in disbelief, scruti-nizing her as if she were some rare bug under his microscope.

"Bits and pieces," she repeated, underscoring the words.

She wouldn't be telling him this unless it was going somewhere, Alex thought. Could he have been wrong about her? Was she really this good, to bring a laptop essentially back from the dead? Did this beauty also have brains and skills far beyond those of mortal men, he wondered, suppressing a smile. He was doing his best to distract himself from the fact that despite everything, he felt an attraction to this woman. And that kind of thing, in this kind of situation, could only get in the way.

He grew annoyed with him for feeling this way— and with her for creating these feelings in the first place.

"And?" he asked, blocking an impatient note.

"And," she echoed, picking up his cadence, "I managed to piece together a few of his emails."

"Which is good because?" he questioned impatiently. Getting information out of her was like pulling teeth, he couldn't help thinking. Did the woman like having him dangle like this while she drew everything out?

Probably, he decided. Why else would she do it?

"Well, for one thing, it gives us the names of a few more of his associates," Valri pointed out. "Hopefully, *they're* still alive and we can question them before someone decides to shut them up permanently, too. If Randy knew what Rogers was working on that got him killed, one of them might know, too."

"So let me get this straight," Alex requested, holding up his hand to stop her flow of words until he could properly process everything. He was still trying to get the cobwebs out of his brain. "You've got names and addresses to go with these emails that you magically pulled up?"

She frowned at the word *magically*, but refrained from commenting on it.

"Wouldn't be telling you this if I didn't." Valri leaned back in her chair and felt her back crack in two places, as if something was finally clicking into place. "Just let me go and splash some water in my face and we'll hit the road."

"Or—"

The single word had her stopping in her tracks. When she turned back around to glance at him, she looked less than thrilled.

"Or?" she questioned.

He finally felt as if he was coming to life. His home-brewed black ooze was only partially responsible. Nothing he liked better than to be closing in on a quarry.

"Or you could just give me the list of names you found and I could hit the road while you went on working your magic on that laptop." He nodded at the scarred device on her desk. "You obviously have more luck this way than being out in the field."

But Valri wasn't buying what he was desperately trying to sell her.

"My list, my terms," Valri informed him. She patted the hip pocket of her jeans, indicating that was where she had placed the list. "I won't be but a minute," she promised.

She was gone five.

Striding back into the squad room, Valri held her breath. She half expected to find Brody's chair empty.

It was.

Incensed, she was about to call out his name, asking the other detectives if any of them had seen which way her so-called partner had gone. But just as she opened her mouth, she saw him, talking to someone she didn't recognize.

Grabbing her jacket from the back of her chair, she made her way over to the two men. The other man said something to Brody and then left. He was gone before she reached her partner.

She *really* wanted to ask him what that was all about, but she bit her lower lip instead. She hadn't reached that level yet, where they could talk to one another, ask casual questions, shoot the breeze and gain a toehold in each other's life.

If she asked now, she would only be being overly nosy in his estimation. That wasn't the image she wanted to convey to him. She wanted him to feel that he could count on her, that she had his back no matter what.

That kind of thing took time.

Brody looked somewhat restless, she noticed. But he did seem to be a little more focused in his appearance than he'd been when he first walked in.

"Ready?" he asked her just before she reached him.

Nodding, she answered, "Let's go."

"I told Carson to tell Latimore that we were going to check out a lead," he told her.

"Carson?" she echoed.

"The guy you looked like you wanted to ask me about," he supplied easily. "He just transferred to Homicide."

"He have a partner?" she asked, wondering if Brody was shopping around in case his own partner decided not to come back.

"Not yet."

She bit her lower lip a little harder. It kept her from asking the obvious.

"Can I see the list?" Brody asked her as they went down the hall to the elevator.

Here, at least, she had the advantage, Valri thought. "When we're in the car."

"You don't trust me?" Alex asked the question as if a negative answer would not just surprise him, it would wound him.

Valri had the feeling that he regarded her like an albatross around his neck. That meant he could easily leave her behind if he had the opportunity.

She was honest with him. "I'm working on it," she answered. "But it takes time to build up trust. You know that."

He murmured something under his breath that she couldn't quite make out. Under the circumstances, she thought that maybe it was better that way.

"Girlfriend?" she asked him out of the blue after several silent moments had gone by.

The elevator had arrived and he stepped in. Where the hell had that come from? "Come again?" he asked.

"The woman you were trying to drink out of your system, was she a girlfriend?" Valri asked. "Or a former girlfriend?"

Alex's eyes swept over her for a moment. Under a different set of circumstances, the woman standing beside him would have aroused his interest. She was quite frankly his type. But she was a Cavanaugh, which meant she was off-limits. Totally.

He laughed. "Hardly," he told her, then asked, "And why are you so curious?"

Valri shrugged. "Just trying to be sympathetic and also to get to know you a little better." She had to start somewhere, didn't she? Valri mused. "After all, we are partners."

"*Temporary* partners," Alex reminded her, emphasizing the word.

"*Everything* is temporary if you look at it a certain way," she pointed out. "We're all only here on this earth temporarily, but it's what we do with that time that counts."

Getting off, they walked toward the rear entrance, where the parking lot was located.

Alex rolled his eyes. "I swear, if you break into a

chorus of 'I Believe,' or some such song, I'm driving off and leaving you here."

She offered him a wide grin. "I'm the one with the addresses, remember?"

It *really* annoyed him that her smile had a way of getting to him. Alex said nothing.

Reaching his car, he got in on the driver's side and slammed his door.

Not trusting Brody to wait for her to get in, Valri flung open the door on her side and all but jumped in quickly.

He started the vehicle while she was buckling up. Gunning the engine, Alex pulled out of the spot with a vengeance, causing her, buckled or not, to lurch forward. Valri braced her hand against the dashboard in front of her, doing her best to remain steady and trying to be in control.

"It was me, wasn't it?" she asked suddenly as the realization occurred to her.

"It was you what?" Alex asked. *Now* what was this thorn in his side talking about?

"It was me you were trying to drink off your mind last night, wasn't it?"

To say her question stunned him would have been an understatement. But he couldn't let her know she was right. It would send an entirely wrong message to her. She'd think he had feelings for her or something equally as preposterous. If there was one thing he had learned about women it was they could take an inch and turn it into a mile.

"You're giving yourself way too much credit," he told her in an offhand manner, hoping that would be the end of it.

"And you're not giving me enough," Valri countered knowingly.

He spared her a glance, then looked straight ahead as he drove. They were not having this conversation, he told himself.

Chapter 8

Valri, however, obviously had different ideas. Like a hungry dog that had stumbled across a bone, she just wouldn't let the topic drop or rest in peace.

She certainly wasn't picking up on the signal he was trying to convey by remaining silent.

"What is it about me that bothers you?" Valri persisted. "Is it because I'm a rookie or because my last name is Cavanaugh?"

Denial was useless, he thought. The woman was a novice, but she wasn't stupid. Even if he had been oblivious to her—and he would have to be dead for that to be true, given her physical attributes—he knew that.

So, after a beat, he finally answered her. "Yes."

"Yes?" Valri echoed. She stared at Alex, waiting for him to elaborate.

Alex merely repeated the word again. "Yes."

And then, in a sudden flash of realization, she got it.

"You're saying yes to both?" Valri questioned.

"You brought it up, not me," he reminded her.

He would have rather left the topic alone altogether. But since she was pressing him for an answer, he wasn't about to lie. His present reaction to her was fueled by both of the things she had mentioned.

"Well, you can't pick your family—although, honestly, if I could, I have to tell you that I wouldn't change anything. I'm proud of being a Cavanaugh and proud of the rest of the family. There isn't a single thing about my family that I'd want to change."

God, he would, Alex thought. If there was such a thing as a do-over in life, a way to petition the higher-powers-that-be, he would have done everything in *his* power to be born into a normal family. Definitely not into one whose members studied art history up close and personal in the privacy of some secluded basement where their stolen goods were stored while deals involving a change of hands were negotiated.

"And as for my being a rookie," Valri continued, addressing what she took to be his second objection to being partnered with her, "as near as I can tell, even God had a first day. My job as a rookie is to learn everything I can from the experienced people around me. People like you," she emphasized. "I'm not going to get in your way, and I have no intentions of holding you back."

She took a breath, coming to what she felt was her most important point. "But I can't learn anything from you if you leave me behind, or take me along but do everything you can to shut me out."

She sounded earnest enough and he believed that *she* believed what she was saying. That led him to ask her a question that had been bothering him.

"Why would you want to risk being out in the field?" Alex asked. "You've got a gift that not that many people have. Hell, people with the kind of talent you have can write their own ticket in this world. Why would you want to even *be* a cop?"

"It's in the blood," she answered.

And then she smiled at him. It occurred to him that it was the sort of smile that men vied for. The kind of smile that was instantly personal no matter what the surroundings were. The kind of smile that men like him had to be wary of.

"My father tried to talk me out of applying to the police academy, told me that I had it in me to become anything I wanted to, and that he didn't want to have to worry every time I walked out of the house wearing dress blues." A distant affection filtered into her smile as she remembered the way it had all played out. "I would have loved to have put his mind at ease, but this is something I have to be."

She looked at Brody. Something told her that they weren't all that different in the way they felt about what they were doing. It wasn't a job, it was a calling.

"The fact that I've got an extensive background in computers gives me something extra to bring to the table. All I ever wanted to do was protect and serve—and occasionally play a video game," she added with a quick—and extremely sexy in its innocence—wink.

And with that, she managed to get to him. She was still a Cavanaugh, still came with an invisible "hands off" sign because of that, but he could totally understand she wanted to use her abilities in order to do something positive in life.

If nothing else, that was how he had felt when he turned eighteen and had decided to rebel against his father and the "family business."

They had labeled him a black sheep, lamenting that he was wasting the "gifts" he had. Things he would have never been able to learn in any school.

Things that he had, for the most part, turned his back on.

"It was you," he finally admitted, answering the question Valri had asked a couple of minutes ago.

"I was the one who drove you to drink?" she asked in disbelief. Even though she had guessed it, hearing him actually confirm her suspicions seemed almost surreal. She couldn't picture anyone reacting to her in that manner for *any* reason. "Why?"

His original objections to having to work with her had just disappeared. But another issue hadn't been cleared up.

"I don't like being in situations I can't control, and I had no say in getting you as a partner, temporary or not." The nature of the job necessitated trusting a partner to have your back. If that was missing from the work relationship, then there was an element of danger to the job that made it that much more difficult.

Valri suddenly saw the whole thing from *his* point of view. She blew out a long breath.

"Wow." And then she watched him for a long moment. She had only one course of action open to her that would alleviate his dilemma. "I can ask the chief to give me another partner."

"You'd do that?" Alex questioned, surprised. He would have thought that she'd do her best to convince him what an asset she would be to him. This was a complete 180 turn on her part.

"Yes," she replied quietly. "I don't want to be the one responsible for you becoming an alcoholic."

He expected her to laugh then. But she didn't. She was serious, he realized. That put an entirely different spin on the way he viewed her. She wasn't behaving like a crown princess.

"You don't have to go to the chief," he told her.

"I thought that was what you wanted," she protested, confused.

"I did," he admitted. "But I don't anymore."

"You're sure?"

He continued looking at the road, stopping just in time for a light that turned red too quickly. "I'm sure," he told her.

"But I don't want you uptight and frustrated."

He couldn't picture having this conversation with Montgomery. Maybe he *was* trading upward. "I'll work it out of my system. It's my problem, not yours. Besides—" he thought of his background for a moment "—I've dealt with far bigger problems than you and managed to keep going."

"What kind of bigger problems?" Valri asked.

Oh no, he wasn't about to talk about his family. That was a step too far as far as he was concerned. "Let's see if we can make some progress with this case, then we'll talk about that." He figured that she'd forget about it eventually.

"Okay. Fair enough," she agreed, then added, "But I'll hold you to it."

He laughed shortly. He couldn't make the mistake of taking *anything* for granted with this live wire. He was quickly learning that she wasn't a thing like what he expected. The woman was going to keep him on his toes. Constantly.

"Never occurred to me that you wouldn't."

"Brody," she began.

"What?" Was she going to argue that point? Or was there something else she wanted to drag out and dissect to satisfy some inner question gnawing away at her?

Valri pointed to something on her right. "We're here."

Alex blinked and looked around, then glanced at the address she had given him. Talking with Cavanaugh had made the miles melt away.

He cleared his throat, parking beside the curb. They were in a residential area. "I knew that," he muttered.

Valri merely grinned, but said nothing.

Getting out of the car, she let her partner lead the way to the front door. The detective had a really nice, tight butt, she caught herself thinking as she came up the short path behind him. She assumed he worked out a lot.

Focus on the case, not on something that's out of reach, she ordered silently just as Brody knocked on the door.

It took a while for the door to finally open. The woman in the doorway had faded red hair and roots that needed work. She smelled of cigarette smoke and anger.

"Detectives Brody and Cavanaugh," Brody said, identifying both of them. He held his ID up for the woman to see. "We're looking for Jason Bigelow."

Mrs. Bigelow regarded them suspiciously for a moment, squinting at the IDs, then pointed them in the right direction.

"Is he in?" Alex asked.

The short, squat woman rolled her eyes. "He's *always* in." It was not a boast but a weary statement of fact.

Almost predictably, Jason Bigelow, the gamer they had come to talk to, lived in a small granny unit that was located behind the main house on his widowed mother's property.

The small, eight-hundred-square-foot quarters where Jason Bigelow lived had a great deal of potential, potential that had gone begging because every waking moment that Jason didn't spend working at his part-time job as a Heavenly Pizza delivery boy he spent sitting in front of his big-screen monitor, fighting three-dimensional tattooed soldiers who had been assimilated by aliens and were out to destroy civilization as the world knew it.

The gamer didn't answer his door at first, even though Alex knocked hard. Impatient, Alex gave up knocking and took out what appeared to be a silver key and something else that resembled a pointed, bent nail file.

When Valri looked at him in question, he told her he was "just making sure Bigelow's okay. Didn't you hear someone cry out for help?"

Amazed that a detective would actually use

that ploy, Valri caught on instantly. She was rather pleased that her new partner wasn't a stickler for protocol and understood that there were times when rules had to be bent and people who mattered had to look the other way in order to save lives.

It always boiled down to saving lives, Valri thought.

"I thought I did, but then I thought that maybe it was my imagination."

"Well," he theorized with a perfectly straight face, "we couldn't have both heard your imagination, now, could we?"

"I guess not," she replied, playing along.

And then she actually heard something once the door was open. A noise that sounded suspiciously like angry cursing. Specifically, very brisk cursing that was being discharged faster than machine-gun fire.

The reason for the volley of expletives was because Jason Bigelow's avatar had been killed in the fourth assault on the territory he was attempting to defend from an infestation of an army of the undead.

"Well, looks like this one isn't dead," Alex commented to her.

"Thank God for that," Valri said, watching the man they had come to question. She was amazed that Bigelow was so absorbed in winning that he didn't even seem to know they were in the room with him.

It wasn't until Alex tapped him on the shoulder that the gamer become aware that he wasn't alone. Startled, caught halfway between the real world and the world that seemed more real to him than his actual existence, Jason held up his controller as if it was some sort of a talisman he could use as a weapon. Thin, slight and of sub-average height, the gamer had longish, dull brown hair that looked as if he had combed it with an eggbeater sometime in the last week. He looked more like one of the characters in the game he was playing than a real, live person.

Scrambling off the sofa, he turned to face the two strangers in his home. "Who are you and what are you doing in my house? My mom send you?" It wasn't a question so much as an accusation. "Is this an intervention?" Not waiting for one of them to confirm or deny his supposition, Jason supplied his own answer. "My God, it *is* an intervention."

His eyes narrowed as he took another long look around. "But aren't there supposed to be more people at an intervention? Where are my friends?" Bigelow demanded.

"Apparently getting killed," Alex told him without any preamble.

Bigelow shrieked, the high-pitched sound ripping through the entire granny unit.

"Killed?" he cried in horror. And then apparently his ghoulish side, the part of Bigelow that had been nurtured by the types of video games he favored, rose to the surface. His eyes almost gleamed as he breathlessly asked, "Who?"

Never taking his eyes off the rather diminutive gamer—if the man claimed to be five-seven he was stretching it—Alex felt around the wall close to the door, looking for a light switch. Locating it, he turned the light on.

The three rather weak overhead lights—there was a fourth one, but the bulb was burnt out—provided less illumination than what was coming from the TV monitor. Combined, they created a somber ambience throughout the room.

"Randy Wills and Hunter Rogers." Valri filled in the names for the gamer.

Jason completely ignored the first name and seemed to instantly home in on the second, more well-known one. The light was poor, but it appeared to Valri that the man's face had gotten a little pale. "The King?" he cried. "He's dead?"

Valri nodded. "I'm afraid he is. Randy seemed to think Rogers was into something that would have gotten him killed. Would you know anything about that, or what it could have possibly been?" When Bigelow looked as if he was about to jump out of his skin, she had her answer. "What was it?" she asked.

Jason looked as if he was one step away from hyperventilating. "I can't say."

The one thing Alex prided himself on was his

ability to read body language. The gamer's fairly screamed that he was lying.

Stepping into Jason's space, he lowered his face to the gamer's and demanded, "Can't or won't?"

Jason looked as if he felt he was trapped. "I can't tell you anything. If they kill me, who'll be there for my mother? She needs me."

Alex exchanged glances with Valri. Ethel Bigelow looked far more capable and down-to-earth than her son did. It wasn't concern for his mother that had the gamer trying to clam up. It was fear of the consequences he was in for if he spoke up.

"Nobody's going to kill you, Jason. If you help us out, we'll put you into protective custody," Alex told him. "You and your mother."

Jason obviously wasn't buying it. "Is that what you did for The King and that other guy you mentioned?" Jason challenged, his voice on the very brink of hysteria. "How'd that work out for them? Huh? Huh?"

"The King was already dead," Valri told him, answering Jason's question before Brody could. She had a feeling that the detective was close to taking the man's head off, and the gamer looked as if he would crumble rather than give them anything useful to work with. "And the other guy, Randy, dragged his feet and waited too long. They got to him before we could do anything. You don't want that happening to you, do you, Jason?"

"No," he nearly cried. "No, I don't. But I don't know that much, really. I always find out about things thirdhand. Nobody tells me anything—they don't think I count," he lamented.

"You count, Jason," she assured him softly. "Tell us what you do know," Valri coaxed. She could see by Brody's face that he thought treating the gamer with kid gloves was a waste of time, but the way she saw it, it was the only angle they could play. Who knew where the next break was coming from?

"I overheard Knik saying that The King was working on perfecting the software for a mobile cell tower."

"Nik?" Alex questioned.

"Knikelson, this hacker that the King let hang around sometimes," Bigelow was quick to fill in.

"Why would this Knik want a mobile cell tower?" Alex asked. He noticed that Valri had grown very quiet. Rather than enjoying the momentary break, her silence made him uneasy.

What she said next made him even more so. "To intercept signals in the area and collect the data that's going back and forth between emails."

"And they'd want this because…?" Alex asked, hoping against hope that the sick feeling in the pit of his stomach was wrong.

With Bigelow whimpering that he was a dead man, Valri continued with her explanation. "A lot of personal information can be gathered from email.

The most common thing, though, would be to find out when a person or a family was going to be away on vacation. That way, the hackers can either charge expensive items on the family's credit cards and have them delivered to the house while the people are away—or they can go the old tried-and-true route, robbing them of their jewelry and their artwork. They break into the house, no muss, no fuss, no civilians to deal with."

Valri had unknowingly struck a nerve with the last scenario. Instantly on his guard, Alex couldn't help wondering if his lucky streak was finally over. He'd gone into homicide thinking that this way, his path was never going to cross the path of any member of his family. They were gifted, conscienceless thieves, but they weren't murderers, that much he was sure of.

Or at least he had been.

He had this nervous feeling that he might have to revise his assessment of the situation.

Oh God, for all their sakes, he fervently hoped not.

"Do you know if he was doing this for someone?" Valri pressed. "From what I remember of The King, he wasn't the type to do this kind of dirty work just for himself."

"He wasn't," Bigelow told her, apparently glad that she understood.

"Then was someone paying him to hack into different systems?" she asked.

"He did it just for the challenge," Bigelow declared, avoiding making eye contact.

"And?" Alex demanded.

"And because he was being paid pretty well." The gamer couldn't say the words fast enough.

"Who was paying him?" Alex asked. His tone of voice made it clear he wasn't about to take any evasive answers.

Frightened, Jason shook his head. "I don't know. I swear on my daddy's grave, I never heard his name."

"Can you make an educated guess, then?" There was no room for any answer other than yes. Alex made that clear.

"Not the name, but—but—but," Jason stuttered, tripping over his tongue, "I think I caught a glimpse of one of the guys as I was leaving The King's place."

"One of the guys," Valri repeated. This was something new. "So there's more than one."

"Couldn't swear to it, but from the way The King talked, it sounded like there were two, maybe three of them. Three, that's right, three of them," he corrected himself. "He referred to them once as the tribunal. I got the impression he didn't like them, but he liked the money, and he liked the idea of putting one over on people in authority. It was his way of thumbing his nose at them, so he did it."

Alex picked up on the tense the gamer used. "Then he did finish the program."

"Oh, yeah. Said it worked like a dream," Bigelow recounted proudly, like a disciple speaking about sitting at the master's knee. "Said he was even thinking of using it a couple of times himself, but he'd have to use their equipment and he didn't think they'd let him." Bigelow shrugged—and then stopped. "Maybe that's even what got him killed," Bigelow cried as the idea suddenly occurred to him.

"And you said you think you saw one of them," Alex said, reminding the gamer what he'd said a minute ago.

"Yeah, maybe," he said, hedging.

"If we put you together with our sketch artist, do you think you could remember enough to work with him?" Alex asked.

"Sure, why not," the gamer agreed like a man who had no other options before him. And then his face lit up like that of a six-year-old when he asked, "On the way to the precinct, can I work the siren?"

All he wanted to do was get the gamer to the police station as quickly as possible with a minimum of fuss, if that was possible.

"Maybe," Alex hedged. "We'll talk."

It was obvious that Bigelow took that as a yes.

Chapter 9

"All I'm saying is that it really didn't hurt anything to let him flip the siren on for a few seconds. And if it put Jason in a more cooperative mood, so much the better," Valri pointed out to her partner. "Right now, that gamer is the closest thing we have to a witness in this case."

Alex shook his head. They had just left the gamer with the precinct's sketch artist, Mara McFadden, a woman who worked in two venues. The first was the old standby: pencil and sketch pad. The second was more complex.

It involved operating a software program that in turn allowed the final "sketch" to be compared against a database filled with the faces of previous offenders. In this case, the group comprised hackers ranging from hardened criminals to budding geniuses who got off pitting themselves against complicated security systems meant to keep the common hacker out.

Alex's attention was focused on the gamer sitting by Mara's desk. "It was like dealing with an overgrown, socially challenged kid."

"No argument there," Valri guaranteed. "But that overgrown kid might provide us with an actual lead, so it's really in everyone's best interest to keep him happy and cooperative."

Alex's deep blue eyes shifted to look at the woman beside him. She was growing on him faster than he would have thought possible. He found himself annoyed at the idea of her availing herself of the company of gamers. She was better than that. How could she have put up with the likes of people like Wills and Bigelow?

The realization that he was reacting like a man and not like a cop suddenly hit him. He needed to get his priorities straight. What his partner did during her free time was her business, not his.

Still, there were questions that begged for input if not actual answers.

"And this was your world?" he asked Valri incredulously.

A smile played on her lips. Looking back, at times she caught herself wondering the same thing.

"Emphasis on the word *was*," she pointed out, keeping her voice low. She didn't want to distract Jason from working with Mara to create a sketch of the man he saw talking to Rogers.

She had aroused his curiosity—he refused to believe that she'd aroused something more as well. Long hours were making him punchy. "What made you stop?" Alex asked.

Valri lifted her shoulders in a quick, dismissive shrug. "I grew up, I guess."

He could accept that. "Good reason."

It took almost an hour before Bigelow was finally satisfied with Mara's rendition of the man he said he'd seen with Rogers. The man who might have been involved in Rogers's murder.

Valri moved in closer to look at the drawing, just in case the man appeared familiar to her.

He didn't.

Mara indicated the sketch. "I'll get this into the system right away. The minute I get a match, I'll notify you," she promised, then looked at the two detectives. "Which one of you is lead on this?"

"He is," Valri said before her partner had a chance to answer the question.

For his part, Alex was surprised that Cavanaugh hadn't just said it was her. After all, *she* was the one with the background in the tech world, and they had never actually spoken outright about who was in charge. He was the one with more time under his belt, but that wouldn't have stopped some people from claiming lead.

Maybe this so-called partnership could work after all, even if she was a rookie and a Cavanaugh to boot. This time, the thought evoked a kind of half smile from him rather than his usual reaction.

"What's your cell number, detective?" Mara asked.

Alex gave her his card. "It's got my cell number on the bottom," he told her. "The other one is the phone on my desk in the squad room."

Mara wrote both down on the edge of her sketch pad and then pocketed the card.

Getting to his feet, Bigelow looked like an elf getting all revved up. "What's next?" he asked them. It seemed obvious that he enjoyed being in the center of things, liked the attention he was garnering. "Next, we send you home," Alex informed the gamer flatly.

Bigelow looked disappointed, and then nervous. He'd made a point, while on the way to the precinct, of telling them how much he loved his solitude, loved getting in touch with people only through the medium of video games. But now the prospect of being alone seemed to frighten him.

"Home? What about that protection you promised?" he demanded, looking from Alex to Valri.

"It'll be there," Valri assured him. The look she spared Alex told the detective that she expected him to back her up and make all this happen. "We're posting a guard outside your mother's house. Most likely," she continued in a calming voice, "nobody even knows you left your gaming console, which means that you have nothing to worry about."

"Yeah, tell that to Wills," Bigelow muttered audibly as Alex signaled to the closest uniformed policeman to come join them.

Valri managed to hide her surprise as she looked at the gamer. "Then you *did* know who I was talking about when I mentioned that Wills was dead, too."

"Yeah, I knew," Bigelow admitted, his tone daring her to make something out of his admission. "I beat him in a tournament once. Real sore loser," Bigelow recalled with a dismissive shake of his head. "Can't say I'm sorry that he's gone, 'cause I'm not." And then something occurred to the gamer. "Hey, now with The King gone, that means that everything's going to be thrown wide open." His small brown eyes were practically shining as he cried, "There's gonna have to be a new king."

And she knew just what the gamer was thinking. But she had a feeling that he wasn't built for long-range strategy.

"You work on your game, Jason," she told him, giving him a pat on his arm. "Officer Callahan here will take you home," Valri said, then turned Bigelow over to the tall, strapping policeman.

"And you actually associated with guys like that?" Alex marveled as Bigelow was being ushered down the corridor toward the elevator.

"For a while," Valri qualified. Looking back, that period of her life almost felt as if it had happened more than a lifetime ago. In reality, it had just been three years in her past.

Wanting to change the subject a little, she regarded Alex and asked, "Now what?"

"Now more legwork," he told her. "How many other names did you manage to recover from Rogers's defunct laptop?"

"Just two others," she admitted, this time taking out the paper with their names and addresses on them and volunteering that to Brody. "But I'm sure there're more," she added. "If I keep at it, trying different recovery programs, I'm pretty sure I can extract at least a few more names."

The expression on her face told Alex that she was bracing herself to hear him tell her to remain here and work on the laptop.

But because she had turned over her one bargaining chip to him—the names and addresses of the other two gamers the deceased had corresponded with—he decided to take her along.

"That'll be your homework assignment," Alex

told her. "For now, why don't we go and talk to those two guys you did find."

Her smile reminded him of sunshine after a long bout of rain. "Sounds like a plan," she agreed.

Before they went to talk to the first name on the two-man list, Alex drove to a fast-food restaurant.

Confused, Valri looked around. This had nothing to do with the two men on the list. "What are we doing here?" she asked.

"Oh, I'd give it a wild guess and say, 'Getting a late lunch.' In case you haven't noticed, we haven't taken a break and we worked right through the morning hours."

"I noticed," she answered. "I just thought that was what you did when you reached detective level."

"Can't have you dropping from hunger your first week as a detective," he told her, guiding his car into the drive-through lane.

Rather than eat on the go, Alex pulled his vehicle into a parking space and turned the engine off. When she eyed him questioningly, all he said was "Compromise." She took it to mean that was his answer to stopping altogether and eating inside the restaurant versus eating on the move.

"Think Bigelow got it right?" Alex asked her as they were both making short work of their cheeseburgers and fries.

Valri held her hand up, indicating that she had

to swallow before answering him. "What do you mean?"

"That 'The King'—" he said the title with an edge of sarcasm in his voice "—created a false cell tower for someone?"

She had already thought that through herself. "It's very possible," she told him.

"Then why kill him?" Alex asked. "Wouldn't he be more valuable to this person or persons alive?"

She'd thought about that, too, and gave Alex her conclusions, such as they were. "Maybe he got greedy and wanted more than he'd been paid. Or maybe they did it to keep him from telling anyone else what they were doing. Rogers wasn't the type to keep quiet," she told Alex.

"Elaborate," Alex coaxed, interested.

"He liked to thump his chest, tell people how smart he was, how good he was. He wasn't humble by any means. That's why he got that nickname. And maybe that was what got him killed," she guessed.

Alex looked at her for a long moment. "I'm having a harder and harder time picturing you involved with people like that," he confessed. The more he got to know her, the less plausible her association with gamers seemed.

"They're not *all* like that," Valri assured him. "But the thing that everyone who's part of that world is, is very competitive." She recalled what it was like signing on for a tournament. "You start out challenging yourself and wind up pitting yourself against everyone else."

The adrenaline high was thrilling at first. But eventually, there was just the tension and it outweighed the thrills.

"After a while, that kind of thing gets old. At least, it did for me." She wiped her hands with a napkin and put that and the empty wrapper into the paper bag that her lunch had come in.

"Were you ever tempted to hack into someone's security system?"

The question came at her out of the blue and caught her completely off guard for a moment. She stared at her partner incredulously.

"I'm a Cavanaugh," Valri pointed out. "We don't do that kind of thing, remember?"

"I didn't ask you if you did it. I asked if you were ever tempted." His eyes held hers. "There's a difference."

"You're asking me if I was ever tempted to hack into a system just to see if I could do it?" She thought that was rather a strange question to ask, but she addressed it seriously. "Sure." She could remember two such instances, but neither had gone beyond idle curiosity. "But there are consequences for anything you do, and satisfying my own sense of curiosity wasn't worth turning my dad's hair gray—not to mention bringing shame to the Cavanaugh name."

"So you took the safe route and became a cop," he concluded, amused.

After finishing his cheeseburger, he crumpled up the wrapper it had come in and deposited it along with the empty French fries container into his paper bag.

"Point taken." Her sunny grin seemed to fill up every single empty space inside the car, bringing warmth along with it.

He caught himself wishing that they weren't working together. That he could just drive to some nice little club with her where they served drinks and bluesy music. Some place where they could talk—or not talk—for hours and maybe even dance together.

Knock it off, he ordered himself.

They had a case to solve and that was his reality right now, not some fantasy he wasn't free to act on.

And that was probably a good thing, he decided. But they were and that was his reality right now. "Time to roll," he announced, starting the engine.

They struck out with the other two gamers, both of whom turned out to be only on the very fringes of the existence that had represented the whole world for the two victims. The two gamers they questioned had been on Rogers's followers list.

"What the hell is a followers list?" Alex asked her as they got back into his car.

He'd let the term slide when the first gamer had used it, but now that the second one had cited it as well, his curiosity was aroused.

Valri was more than familiar with the term. "Think of it as a groupie list. Once upon a time, only big movie stars had a following. Now everyone who's been in the limelight for ten seconds has one. What with Facebook and Twitter social media and all the other ways of instant mass communications, people can acquire professions of love or hate in the blink of an eye. The people doing the 'professing' are followers."

Alex shook his head. "That can't be a good thing."

"Oh, but it can," she argued. At best, these followers were harmless. At their worst, they became stalkers. "The problem is that every good thing has a bad side to it."

Alex couldn't have agreed more.

"I did it," Shamus Cavanaugh—former police chief and present CEO of a thriving home security company that he ran with the occasional help of his oldest son—declared as he walked into Andrew Cavanaugh's kitchen.

It was a known fact that if Andrew, the former Aurora police chief, was home, there was more than a 90 percent chance of finding him in his kitchen, creating something new out of old standbys.

Today was no different.

Andrew had had his back to his father when the latter had burst in.

"Did what, Dad?" Andrew asked. When it came to his father, Andrew never knew just what to expect, or what the man was up to. The family patriarch was nothing if not unpredictable. *Dull* was definitely not a word that could ever be associated with the older man.

"Joined the French Foreign Legion," Shamus cracked, then said impatiently, "What do you *think* I did?"

"I haven't a clue, Dad. That's why I asked," Andrew replied calmly, pondering what ingredient his version of Hungarian goulash was missing. While it was tasty, something was off and he just couldn't put his finger on it.

"I asked her."

That caught Andrew's attention more than his father's loud entrance.

"Her?"

Andrew had a strong suspicion he knew who his father was referring to, but he wanted to be sure. He understood the danger of making an assumption that, in the end, wasn't correct. His father's moods changed as quickly as eastern weather patterns.

"Lucy. Noelle O'Banyon's grandmother," he said, mentioning the name of the latest woman who had joined the family by marrying one of their own. "I *asked* her," he repeated, emphasizing what to him was the most important word.

Before his son could express his surprise—or demand to know what the hell he was thinking, getting married again at his age—Shamus was quick to head him off.

"I figured I wasn't getting any younger, but I wasn't dead yet either, and hell, what did I have to lose? Your mother, God rest her soul, died a long time ago and I got used to that empty space inside of me. But after I met Lucy—and we hit it off right from the start—I realized that it didn't have to be that way. That space didn't have to stay empty. So I asked her," he concluded proudly.

Andrew let the goulash take care of itself and turned around to face his father squarely. He needed to get something cleared up. "Asked her to marry you or just to move in with you?"

Shamus scowled at his firstborn. "I wouldn't insult a lady like Lucy by asking her to shack up with me," he said indignantly.

"No offense, Dad," Andrew said in apology because he knew that was what his father was waiting to hear, "but you are unpredictable." *Loose cannon* was a more apt description for the man, but Andrew kept that to himself. It would only get his father incensed. "I take it by that big grin on your face that she said yes."

"She did, son. She did, indeed," Shamus said happily, sounding every bit like a teenager in love for the first time. If he grinned any harder, his face might be in danger of splitting in half. "Lucy and I want you to throw the reception together for us."

Andrew wouldn't have had it any other way. He loved any excuse for getting the family together to celebrate something.

"Sure, I'd love to," he told his father. "Have you two set a date?" he asked, moving over to the calendar that was hanging on the wall.

"Next Saturday," Shamus replied.

Andrew turned to look at his father, certain that he had to have heard wrong. "*Next* Saturday? You're kidding, right?"

Shamus frowned and eyed his oldest as if his son was not connecting the dots here.

"I did mention that I'm not getting any younger, didn't I?" It was a rhetorical question. "Now that I found someone I want to spend the rest of my life with, I don't want to waste any time. There's not as much of 'the rest of my life' left as I'd like, so I'm not waiting any longer than I absolutely have to. I already got in touch with a priest. Father Gannon said he's free on that day, so he'll marry us." He narrowed his eyes, pinning his son down. "Now, can we have the reception here, or are we going to have to hold it in the precinct parking lot?"

Andrew rolled his eyes heavenward. His father could go utterly dramatic on him at the drop of a hat. "You don't have to have it in the precinct parking lot, Dad. I can have it here. It's just a little short notice, that's all."

Shamus clapped his oldest son on the back. "I've got great faith in you, boy. When it comes to a party, no one throws it together better than you do. We just have to get the word out, that's all."

"Get the word out about what?" Rose Cavanaugh asked as she walked into the kitchen, drawn there by the sound of voices as well as to check on her husband's progress with dinner.

"Rose, my beautiful, darling Rose," Shamus cried, taking both her hands in his and all but dancing about the room with the youthful-looking blonde. "You're getting a new mother-in-law."

Accustomed to her father-in-law's less than run-of-the-mill behavior, Rose still stopped dead in her tracks and stared at the man.

"Excuse me?"

"You're getting a new mother-in-law," Shamus repeated gleefully, then happily added, "I'm getting married."

Stunned, Rose glanced toward her husband for confirmation, not really expecting any. When Andrew nodded, her jaw dropped.

"Dad popped the question to Noelle's grandmother, Lucy."

The years had taught Rose Cavanaugh to take everything that came her way, large or small, in stride.

After having gone missing herself for eleven years due to a car accident that had left her with amnesia, and then nearly losing her husband to a serial killer a little more than a year ago, everything else, she felt, could be dealt with.

And that went double when it came to a certain happy man in his late seventies. "So when's the big day, Dad?" she asked.

"Saturday," Shamus told her.

Well, maybe not *everything*, she silently amended. She stared at her father-in-law, dumbfounded. The man was an endless source of surprises not just to her, but to everyone else in the family.

"Really?"

Again, her husband, Andrew, was her source of confirmation as well as her veritable rock. "Really," he told her.

"Wow" was the first word out of Rose's mouth. For the moment, she didn't trust herself to say anything else. And then she grinned at her father-in-law.

"Congratulations, Dad. I guess this is when you have that son-father talk with him," she said, glancing over at her husband. Rose didn't even attempt to keep a straight face as she said that.

But Andrew merely shook his head. "There is nothing that *anyone* can tell my father. Ever."

"And don't you forget it," Shamus agreed, winking at his daughter-in-law. At the moment, he deemed himself to be the happiest man on earth.

Chapter 10

When her cell phone rang the next morning an hour after she'd gotten to work, Valri was aware that the call could be coming from any one of a number of people. She wasn't exactly a recluse and had her share of friends, not to mention the fact that she had far more relatives who had her cell number than the average three people put together.

However, for the most part, if her phone rang during her work hours, more likely than not it was something that had to do with her job.

But even keeping all this in mind, Valri was completely caught off guard by her caller.

She answered her cell on the third ring, identifying herself in her most professional voice.

"Cavanaugh."

There was a pause on the other end. When she received no response, she thought that the caller was a wrong number, or that the signal had been dropped. In either case, she didn't have time to waste on someone who wasn't identifying himself or herself.

About to terminate the call, she heard a very deep, resonant voice ask, "Valri?"

The voice was vaguely familiar, but she couldn't immediately place it.

Her cautious "Yes?" had Alex looking up at her from his desk.

So far, she had gotten no further with resurrecting the data on the smashed laptop and they were planning to go out to canvas Rogers's neighborhood in a few minutes. The idea at this point was to show the sketch that Mara had given them around and hope someone recalled seeing the man.

Alex saw the confusion on her face.

"Problem?" he asked her, his eyes indicating the cell phone in her hand.

Since she couldn't answer Alex directly, she raised and lowered her shoulders to indicate that she hadn't a clue if the person on the other end of the call could be categorized as a problem or not.

The next moment, she had her answer as the man on the other end of the line identified himself.

"Valri, this is Andrew Cavanaugh. I'm not interrupting anything, am I?" the man asked.

"*Chief* Andrew Cavanaugh?" she asked in disbelief. Out of the corner of her eye she could see that she had managed to capture her partner's full attention now. He started listening intently.

"I'd rather you thought of me as Uncle Andrew, actually," Andrew told her with a kindly laugh punctuating his statement.

"Yes, Chief. I mean—"

Valri pressed her lips together as she upbraided herself. She was tripping over her own tongue, trying to be respectful and still addressing him according to the man's wishes.

What was wrong with her? It wasn't as if she hadn't ever spoken to the man before. She had. Several times. But the exchanges had been face-to-face and exceedingly brief in nature. Talking to him on the phone somehow seemed to change those parameters.

"That's all right," Andrew assured her gently. "You can call me anything you're comfortable with. I'll get right to the point. The reason I'm calling is that I need your help."

"*My* help?" she asked, practically stuttering. She couldn't think of a single thing that she could do for the former chief of police that either he or someone in his more immediate family couldn't do first and most likely better.

"I'm afraid so," he confirmed. "My brother Brian tells me that you are an absolute wizard when it comes to dealing with anything involving technology, say like the social media."

Instead of making the reason for his call understood, his request created more complications. Maybe if she asked a few questions, this would get clearer for her.

"You want me to set up a Facebook page for you?" Valri asked, making what was probably a wild guess—although the man had mentioned social media, so who knew? Maybe he was sticking his toe in, testing the waters before he made up his mind one way or another.

His laugh, deep, warm and hearty, instantly shot down her theory.

"No, no, nothing like that," he told her when he finally stopped laughing. "Here's the situation—I need to notify a large number of people about an event taking place this Saturday and I need to do it as soon as possible."

Valri had already grabbed a pencil and had begun making notes on the first piece of paper she found the instant the former chief of police had said he needed her help.

The scenario he'd just painted had her instantly trying to come up with a satisfying answer she thought that the man could work with. "Well, a

Facebook page could take care of that for you," she theorized.

"What if they don't all have that?" he asked, then added, "Facebook pages," to clarify what he was asking. "Isn't there some other way?"

She hadn't thought of someone not having a Facebook page. All the people she knew did, even if they only glanced at it once in a while.

"Good point," she responded. Half a second later, she had another possible solution to the man's problem. "There's Twitter social networking. We could send out a mass message that way."

More silence, which told her that the chief was giving her solution some thought. Glancing up at Alex, she saw that he was continuing to watch her as if he could glean things from her side of the conversation and her body language.

"What if some of these people don't Twitter?" Andrew asked.

Valri grinned, but felt it best not to correct the chief about the proper terminology just yet. The last thing she wanted was for the man to think she was trying to undermine him.

"As long as they have a cell phone," Valri assured her great-uncle, "I can get the message to them."

"Sounds good," Andrew responded enthusiastically. "I knew you'd come up with a solution."

Valri was surprised how good that simple compliment made her feel.

"I could work up a list of people and get that to you—" the chief was saying.

"I could stop by your house this evening, sir, and pick it up," she offered.

"No, no reason for you to go any more out of your way than you already will be. I'll have some-one from here drop the list off as soon as I'm done with it. They'll leave it on your desk in the squad room if that's all right with you."

"Sure, fine," she agreed, then felt compelled to ask, "You know where I am?"

Her surprise was greeted with another gentle laugh. "Valri, I'm the former chief of police. I *re-tired* from the force, I didn't die. I know where ev-eryone in the family is. Oh, by the way, keep this Saturday open," he told her.

"Of course, sir," she instantly agreed. And then her curiosity got the better of her. "If you wouldn't mind telling me, why am I keeping it open?"

"Because, if you agree to come, you'll be attend-ing your first Cavanaugh wedding. I'll get back to you about the list," Andrew promised her. The next moment, he was gone.

She stared at the phone in her hand even though her great-uncle was no longer there. It seemed that even the older generation moved fast, she mused. Valri returned her cell phone to her back pocket.

"Okay, what was all that about?" Alex asked her the moment she had tucked away her phone.

Valri looked up at him, still a little dazed and slightly dumbfounded by what had just transpired. "The chief just asked for my help."

"I figured that part out for myself," he told her. "Just what did the chief of Ds say?"

Valri blinked, then realized the error. "No, not him, the other one." The puzzled expression on Alex's face told her she wasn't making herself clear. But then, she was really still a little muddled herself. It wasn't every day that the former chief of police singled her out and called, asking for her help of all things.

"What other one?" Alex asked. As far as he was concerned, she was talking in riddles.

"The chief of police," she told him. "The *former* chief of police," she emphasized, then, frustrated that she was still coming across as if her brain had just been fried and then scrambled, she amended her amendment and declared, "*Andrew* Cavanaugh."

Alex frowned slightly, trying to follow what his partner was saying. "I thought he'd retired."

"He did," she acknowledged.

"Then why?"

"This is a personal matter," Valri quickly added, making the distinction.

"Oh." He took that to mean that the subject was off-limits to everyone else. "Okay." He tactfully backed away from the matter. "Ready to go?" he asked. "Or do you have to dash out of here in compliance with whatever this personal matter is?"

She tried to read between the lines. Was he annoyed, envious or just amused by all this? She decided not to let it worry her. All she could do was play it as straight as she could and not give her partner any cause to ask for a transfer.

Using various links and connections, she'd managed to find out a few things about her partner. She'd also discovered there was next to no information about his parents or family. She thought it odd, but then, not everyone was born a Cavanaugh with an open book for a life.

"No, this doesn't require any dashing," she assured him. "I'm ready to go if you are."

In response, Alex pushed back his chair and got to his feet. "Then let's get to it."

"You're not going to ask?" she said as they went down the corridor to the elevator.

"Ask what?" He pressed the down button.

"What the chief—what Uncle Andrew," she corrected, thinking it might be easier for Brody to follow what she was saying if she used the man's name instead, "wants me to do."

The elevator arrived almost immediately. Alex waited for her to get on first. Following Valri on, he pressed the button for the first floor. "You said it was personal."

And that was his reason? Wasn't the man human? she wondered.

"I know, but aren't you the least bit curious?" Valri asked.

"What good would it do?" he asked. "I'm assuming that since you didn't immediately volunteer the information on your own, you either can't, or won't. You were probably told to keep it under wraps."

"Actually, Uncle Andrew *didn't* tell me anything specific, other than to keep Saturday open because there was going to be a wedding."

"A wedding?" he echoed. They got off on the first floor. "Whose?"

"Don't know yet," she confessed. "But one of the two is a Cavanaugh."

"Well, that narrows things down," he commented sarcastically.

Valri spread her hands wide. "That's all I know, except that Uncle Andrew wants to notify a lot of people about it." She thought for a second, then asked, "Who do you think it is?"

Alex shook his head. "Sorry, I'm not very up on your family."

She sighed. "It's an awful thing to admit, but neither am I. I mean, I know it's not anyone from my branch of the family, but that's where it stops. I'm still in the process of learning everybody's names."

"Well, that makes you one up on me," he freely admitted.

"Have you heard any rumors?" she asked, still trying to guess who her new uncle was going to be holding a reception for.

"None I can think of. I don't pay attention to rumors. By the way," Alex continued as they made their way to where he'd parked his car this morning, "I think you should know that I can only really focus on one thing at a time. Pull anything more into the mix and I don't always do my best work."

Reaching the vehicle, Valri stared at him over the roof of his car, surprised. "You're actually admitting that?"

Maybe he shouldn't have, he thought. It wasn't exactly 100 percent true. He could concentrate on more than one thing at a time, but when he did, his laser-like focus lost a little of its sharp edge. And the last thing he wanted to be distracted with was something dealing with the Cavanaughs' social life.

"Yeah, why?"

She sat in the shotgun seat and secured her seat belt. "Most guys I know—and I'm referring mostly to my brothers and my male cousins—would rather die than admit that they can't multitask."

"Well, I'm not 'most guys,'" he told her, getting in himself. He buckled up, then added, "And multitasking is highly overrated."

Valri grinned at him, amused. "I believe that *that* is otherwise known as sour grapes."

"Believe whatever you want," Alex told her with a careless shrug. "It's a free country."

She smiled, settling back in her seat as Alex turned his key in the ignition. "Amen to that," she said in reference to his last words.

Some five hours later, they got back into his car, soul-wrenchingly weary with absolutely nothing to show for it.

"Well, that was a colossal waste of time," Alex said to her in disgust.

They had knocked on a total of twenty-three doors in what had until recently been Hunter Rogers's neighborhood. They wound up speaking to a total of eleven different people—the rest had either not been home, or pretended not to be and didn't come to answer their doors.

None of the eleven they *did* speak with had anything to tell them. It seemed that none of the former gamer/hacker's neighbors recognized the man in the drawing. There hadn't even been one who hesitated before saying that the man in the sketch was unfamiliar.

"Think we got it wrong?" Valri asked, looking down at the sketch she'd shown to people over and over again. Belatedly, she buckled her seat belt around her.

About to start up the car, Alex left the key where it was and looked at her. "What do you mean?"

Maybe she was off base about this, but then what were partners for if not to use as sounding boards for half-gelled ideas?

"Maybe Bigelow hadn't recalled the guy's features accurately," she ventured, then looked at Alex to see if he thought she was completely wrong.

But all Alex did was remind her that in a good many cases, "Eyewitnesses are notoriously inaccurate."

"Yes, but Bigelow was so positive." Valri recalled watching the gamer when Mara had completed the sketch. The gamer had all but crowed that she'd gotten it dead-on.

"*Especially* when they're so positive," Alex underscored.

Valri blew out a long, frustrated breath. She knew what this meant. They were back to square one, and she hated that.

"So now what?" she asked as he turned his key and the car came to life.

"Now we go back and I watch you try to communicate with the dead." When Valri looked confused, he laughed and said, "Otherwise known as extracting information from a laptop someone had committed computer-icide on."

That was always an option, she thought, and true to her stubborn nature, she hadn't given up on the laptop yet. But that was extremely slow going and she wanted to do something *now.*

Valri decided to couch her desire to do something other than sit at her desk in language that was more acceptable to the male of the species. "That doesn't sound like much fun for you," Valri told him.

"And banging your head against a brick wall is fun for you?" It was obvious that *that* was how he saw her working with the smashed laptop: as a basic experiment in futility.

Valri thought his words over, then shook her head. His metaphor wasn't accurate. "It's not a brick wall," she told him. "It's plasterboard and in my experience, limited though it is, there's usually something hiding right behind plasterboard."

Her late mother's cousin was in construction and one summer she and a couple of her brothers had worked with him, renovating an old house for extra money. Life had been a lot less complicated then, she thought wistfully. But then, there'd been no pitting herself against the criminal element to get her blood racing, either.

"Hiding?" Alex asked.

It was the thoughtful way that Alex said the word that caught her attention. "What are you thinking?" she asked.

Her question surprised him. Was he that transparent? Or had she gotten that good at reading him so fast? Neither answer was acceptable to him, but the second one was also rather unnerving, as well.

"That maybe we're approaching this from the wrong angle," he finally answered.

"And the right angle is…"

Instead of answering her, he asked a question. "Who would benefit from what Rogers came up with?"

"You mean a way to create a false mobile cell tower?" she asked, quoting what Bigelow had claimed. Again, they were going by what the man had told them. How did they know he was telling the truth?

Alex merely nodded in response to her question.

"Bigelow didn't disagree when I said that the email information was being gathered to find out who was going away on vacation and leaving their homes unattended," Valri reminded him.

"You're right." That was what had been gnawing at him. He thought he was off base, but since she seemed to be agreeing with him, this avenue certainly merited a little more investigating. "Maybe we should find out if there's been a rash of break-ins and burglaries in some of the more wealthy neighborhoods of Aurora." He'd read about there being three the day the chief had paired him up with Cavanaugh. Maybe there were even more.

"What about the security systems?" she asked. "Wouldn't the people going on vacation be arming their security systems before leaving?" she pointed out. It seemed like common sense to her.

Alex waved away her words as easily as one of the thieves they were trying to uncover might have silenced the alarm on the security systems.

"My guess is that disarming those systems is child's play for the guy or guys we're looking for."

"You're probably right."

"Of course I'm right," Alex said, sparing her a glance as they finally began to drive back to the precinct. "All these thieves would need is one person with your kind of aptitude to have computer programs do their bidding and they could most definitely write their own tickets."

She looked at him, completely confused. "Is that a compliment or an accusation?"

He laughed shortly. "If you have to ask, then I guess it didn't make the grade as a compliment."

"Oh, but it did," she responded, a smile curving her generous mouth. "I just had to home in on what you were actually saying."

Before he knew what was happening, her smile had melted right into him, taking no prisoners.

Except for him.

He *had* to stop looking at that mouth of hers, Alex told himself. Not to mention that he had to remember that no matter how attracted he might be to her—and that particular factor kept insisting on growing—Valri Cavanaugh was strictly off-limits.

And he had to keep reminding himself of that

permanently—unless the chief of Ds decided to place her elsewhere.

He'd been better off when all he had been dealing with were issues about being partnered with her.

Chapter 11

When they crossed the threshold of the squad room less than half an hour later, Valri saw someone she thought was familiar standing by her desk. It was the woman's hair that first caught her attention. The mane was as close to flaming red as humanly possible without any chemical help coming from a hair-dye product.

From what she could make out, the woman in question had just dropped something off on her desk and was about to walk away.

Lengthening her stride in order to catch up to the woman, Valri called out her name to get her attention. "Noelle, wait up."

The latter turned around, surprised and pleased to see her approaching. The next moment, Detective Noelle O'Banyon wrapped her arms around her, giving her a heartfelt hug.

"Hey, I just heard about you making the big leagues," Noelle said with genuine enthusiasm. "Congratulations!"

Taking a step back from Noelle, Valri slanted a look toward Brody. For once, he didn't seem annoyed about the reference to their partnership. Maybe the idea was growing on him. She could only hope.

"It's not permanent yet, but I've got my fingers crossed," Valri confided to the woman who had so effortlessly captured her brother Duncan's heart.

"You'll get it," Noelle told her. "Just keep working your magic. Speaking of which, Uncle Andrew had me bring over the list of people he wants you to notify—I supplied the phone numbers," she added. "Trust me, it was faster that way."

Picking up the paper, Valri glanced over the lengthy sheets. There were an awful lot of names. "Is this for your wedding?" she asked the other woman.

They were almost the same height and Noelle's eyes met hers. "Mine? Oh no, ours is going to be around Christmas." Her smile turned into a very wide, very pleased grin, the kind people wore when they suddenly realized that they were the proud guardian of a sensational secret. "Didn't the chief tell you?"

"No. To be honest, I think he forgot," Valri confided.

But Noelle shook her head. "That man doesn't forget *anything*," Noelle assured her. "Now that I think about it, I think that he wanted me to be the one to tell you—I get such a huge kick out of it, even though I haven't completely gotten used to the idea. But then," she added with a good-natured shrug, "I've only known for less than a day."

She paused for a moment to bring more attention to her announcement. "My live wire of a grandmother, Lucy, is marrying the Cavanaugh family's patriarch."

Valri blinked. She was still getting used to who was whom and their positions in the very overwhelming branch of the family that had been uncovered.

"You're going to have to be a little more specific than that. Which one is considered the patriarch?" she asked her future sister-in-law.

"The oldest one," Alex very calmly put in.

Both women turned to look at him, as if they had completely forgotten he was there.

After they'd walked in and the two women began interacting, he realized that they had a bit of history. Alex sensed that this would take a bit of time.

Rather than say anything, he'd just sat down at his desk to wait it out.

"Oh, I forgot to introduce you," Valri said, embarrassed. "Sorry." The word was addressed to both of them. "Brody, this is Detective Noelle O'Banyon. She's in the vice squad and she's going to be my very lucky brother Duncan's wife. Noelle, this is Detective Alex Brody." She looked at him and flashed an appreciative smile. "Brody's teaching me the ropes."

"Struggling not to tie her up in them at times," Alex added, leaning over his desk to shake Noelle's hand.

"I think Duncan expressed a similar sentiment when we first started working together," Noelle told the duo as she returned Alex's firm handshake.

"So who exactly is getting married?" Valri asked, wanting to get this completely clear. As far as she knew, Andrew, Brian and Sean, the older generation's three brothers, were all married.

"Shamus." Noelle inclined her head toward Alex, giving him a further explanation. "He's the chief's father."

The man was also the older brother of Valri's late grandfather. "I was really surprised, though, when I found out that Lucy and Shamus wanted to have the ceremony this Saturday. I tried to talk her into going a little slower, taking the time to do it up right. I told her that there wasn't *that* much of a hurry. Lucy just stared at me with the knowing look of hers, waiting for me to finish. When I did, she said, 'Just wait until *you* leave the comfort of your fifties and sixties. Every second that goes by is one more second you don't have anymore.'" Realizing that she was getting a little misty, Noelle cleared her throat and pulled herself together. "Anyway, I'm glad she's happy." She nodded at the papers she'd dropped off. "Thanks for handling this for her."

Valri was more than happy that she'd been asked to help. "Hey, what's family for if not to help out?" she asked with a warm smile.

"I'm beginning to find that out," Noelle answered— and she was. "See you at the wedding."

"Count on it," Valri promised happily. She found herself growing excited at the very prospect of attending the wedding.

When Noelle left, Alex sat up a little straighter, managing to catch a glimpse of the list the other woman had dropped off, albeit the glimpse *was* upside down.

He let out a low whistle, which in turn caught Valri's attention. "Those are a lot of names," he commented. "That's going to take you forever."

She'd already gotten a head start on this, reviewing mentally what needed to be done. She scrutinized the list now. "Actually, it isn't. I worked up a program for that."

"Of course you did," he quipped. The woman was unbelievable. Beauty and an abundance of brains were one hell of a combination. "Tell me, Cavanaugh, if you got left out in the rain, would you rust?"

"You don't have to be a machine to come up with programs," she pointed out, letting his comment roll off her back.

Picking up the papers, she went down the extensive list quickly, focusing on the surnames that were *not* identical to hers. When she reached the one she was looking for, she grinned. Andrew Cavanaugh was uncanny. He really *was* up on everything that was currently happening.

Looking up again, her eyes met Alex's. "I wouldn't make any plans for Saturday, either, if I were you."

He eyed her suspiciously. "Why?"

"Because you're invited," she informed him gleefully.

"I don't even know the 'happy couple,'" he protested.

She was beginning to get a handle on the way Andrew Cavanaugh and the others operated. "It doesn't matter if you do or don't. You know me and from what I've learned about these blowout parties, that's all it takes. This makes you officially a 'friend' of the family, not to mention that you're also a cop— two reasons for you to be included."

She paused for a second, studying the names on the list. She could reach them all using Twitter, but that took for granted that everyone checked their smartphones several times a day.

"This might actually be simpler if I also post a notice in the break room on every floor." She rolled the thought over in her mind, then decided, "I'll do it. I'll do both." She grinned as she glanced back at Alex. "Better to wear suspenders and a belt than to risk having your pants fall down."

Alex stared at her. "Is that some kind of a Cavanaugh proverb?"

"No, it's just something that my mother used to say," she told him, adding, "She was a very protective lady."

"Protective, huh?" All he could think of was that if the woman *was* protective, then life had to be a living hell for Valri's mother. "She must have had a fit when all of you dutifully marched off to become part of the police department."

"My mother passed away before any of that happened," Valri told him quietly.

"Oh." Alex quickly went into damage-control mode, first removing the size-eleven foot from his mouth. "I'm sorry. I didn't know."

"Why should you?" she asked, absolving him of all guilt. "Don't apologize. It's okay. I don't mind talking about her. In a way, talking about her kind of keeps my mother alive for me."

She looked at Brody for a moment. He was coming around, she realized. That chip he'd had on his shoulder when they first met in the chief's office was mercifully becoming nonexistent.

"How about you?" she asked. "Are your parents alive?"

He appeared a little uncomfortable, and she wondered why.

The next moment, the questions that were being raised in her head had to be put on the back burner. Latimore had emerged from his office and he was heading straight for their desks.

"You might have just caught another one," the lieutenant said, handing Alex a sheet of paper with hastily jotted-down information, including an address, on it.

"Another dead gamer?" Alex asked before he took note of the address where the body was discovered.

"No." The address belonged to a very exclusive residential area where guesthouses came with a million-dollar price tag and main residences were affordable only to approximately one percent of the population. "But it looks like this case might ultimately be connected to our dead hacker."

Alex looked at the address. "What, he came back from the dead and killed someone with blue blood?"

The lieutenant frowned at Alex's irreverent attitude. "This might tie in with that theory you were spinning earlier, the one about the mobile cell tower picking up intel about which houses would be empty because the residents were gone on vacation."

Latimore quickly gave them a thumbnail sketch of the events. "A vacationing couple got into a knockdown, drag-out fight and came back early, ready to call separate divorce lawyers. When they walked in, they surprised the burglar who was lifting a Monet off their wall. From the sketchy details, I gather there was a physical fight. Somehow the husband got hold of the burglar's gun and shot him."

"How bad?" Alex asked.

"As bad as it gets," Latimore answered. "The burglar's dead, the husband's in shock and yelling his head off and the wife is hysterical. It's a noise-fest. Get over there and see if you can get us some kind of answers," the lieutenant ordered.

Alex blew out a breath, then sat up. "Sounds like a perfect way to end the day." He looked over at Valri as Latimore went back to his office. "Listen, you've got that thing to do for your uncle. Why don't you go do it? I can handle this alone."

"I'm sure you can," she agreed. "But I'm coming with you. And since you'll be the one driving, I can get started on Andrew's list while you bring us to the crime scene. I multitask, remember?"

Alex shook his head, but it was because he was amused, not annoyed. "How could I forget? I've got you to remind me."

Valri flashed him a cheerful smile.

He was having less and less luck blocking that out, he thought.

Quail Hill Community prided itself on the high caliber of residents the development attracted. To have something like a burglary/murder—even one in self-defense—happen here was unheard of. Like a true train wreck, it had drawn out almost all of the nearby residents. They gathered, dressed in their designer clothes and overpriced sunglasses, on the outer perimeters of the yellow tape, eager for details while doing their best not to appear that way.

Considering that the crime scene investigation unit, as well as a detective from Robbery, was already on the scene, finding somewhere to park nearby was a feat that was beginning to look next to impossible.

Eventually Alex found a space by the curb that was exactly the length of his vehicle and not an inch more. It was a definite test of his parallel parking skills.

Valri was about to suggest trying farther up the block, but her partner looked determined to get into the small space. She held her tongue as well as her breath.

To her utter amazement, Alex managed to get his car in between two parked SUVs. It took him only one try and he managed to get his vehicle in between the other two without so much as touching either of them.

When he finally released the steering wheel, Valri let out a low, appreciative whistle. Alex looked at her quizzically, half expecting a wisecrack to come out of her mouth.

Instead, she said, "I'm impressed. I couldn't do that," she told him honestly.

He would have been better off if she'd made some sort of sarcastic remark. This softer, gentler version of her was making life very difficult for him. There was nothing there to be annoyed with, nothing to help him remember to keep her at arm's length—especially when he wanted to do something entirely different with his arms.

"You're a Cavanaugh," he told her gruffly as he got out on his side. "You can do anything."

"You know, you're going to have to stop that if we're going to be working together."

"Oh, but I have such few things to look forward to," he quipped melodramatically.

"You have the wedding on Saturday to look forward to," she reminded him crisply, raising the yellow crime scene tape that was stretched before the front of the house, which looked as if it deserved the title "mansion" rather than "house." Impressive in its sleek, clean lines, it still looked exceedingly uninviting to her. She couldn't imagine children playing in a house like this.

"I'm not going," Alex told her. It was a lot safer that way. The last thing he needed was to see this woman in civilian clothing, especially if it hugged her curves—and he had a feeling that it would.

"You *not* going would insult a lot of people," she warned matter-of-factly. "I wouldn't do it if I were you."

He waved a dismissive hand at her words. "With the crowd that'll be coming, those people you think I'll be insulting won't even know that I'm not there."

"Trust me, Andrew will know—and so will Brian. They just have this knack," she assured him, repeating what she'd heard. "They're good people." That much she knew firsthand. "You don't want to be insulting them. Think about it," she coaxed. "The music's always good, the food's even better. It'll be a cop-fest as well as a wedding. There's no reason not to go—unless you want to be ornery," she said, her eyes holding his to see if she'd gotten through to him. "I wouldn't recommend being ornery if I were you. It's really counterproductive and it's not projecting the kind of image you want to cast."

"How do you know all this?"

"I'm a student of human nature as well as a gamer and a cop."

"Detective," he corrected her. "Not cop. There's a difference."

"I'll try to keep that in mind," she promised.

"Now, about you coming to the wedding…" She allowed her voice to trail off, waiting for an answer.

"I'll think about it," he told her. "That's the best I can do right now."

"Think hard," Valri recommended.

They had reached the front door, which was standing wide open.

Valri paused to put paper booties on over her shoes, the kind that medical personnel favored in the operation room. Alex followed suit and wound up leading the way inside.

A tall, slender woman who more than faintly resembled his partner looked up in their direction when he and Valri came closer.

Another cousin, Alex assumed, glancing from the other woman to the one half a step behind him. "One of yours?" he asked, asking the question in a low voice and nodding toward the woman he'd just spotted.

"Depends on whether or not I feel like acknowledging her," Valri replied, a half smile playing along the corners of her lips.

The sound of voices—especially *her* voice—had the woman turning around. Her face lit up the second she looked at Valri.

"Ah, my favorite little geek," the woman said as she crossed to them quickly, a hostess welcoming guests who were late to the table. But her immediate focus was on Valri. "What are you doing away from your computer? If they let you out to get some fresh air, this is definitely *not* the place to do it."

Exercising patience, Valri waited her sister out. Kelly eventually ran out of steam.

"Thanks for your concern, Kelly. Brody," she said, turning toward her partner, "this is Kelly Cavanaugh—one of my sisters. Possibly the most annoying one, but the jury's still out on that."

He ignored the introduction beyond the woman's name. It was best that way. "Nice to meet you," he said, shaking Kelly's hand. The woman appeared to be at least half a head taller than his partner, if not more so.

Because the case had first been called in as a home invasion, Kelly and her partner, Amos, had gotten the case assigned to them. But once the rest of the details came to light, Kelly had called her captain and told the man that the case had turned into one for the homicide squad.

"Is this your first case?" Kelly asked her sister, fully expecting the latter to say yes.

She was surprised when Valri answered, "No, we're already working a homicide case, but there's a chance that this one just might be connected to it."

"Elaborate," Kelly requested.

But Valri didn't want to just lay everything out for her sister—especially when some of the suppositions might turn out to be wrong.

"When we work out the details, I'll let you know," Valri promised.

She turned toward Brody to get his thoughts on whether or not he felt that this latest development was all part of one and the same case the way she did.

Brody had left her talking to her sister while he took stock of what had happened. He made his way over to the body that was still lying facedown on the floor. Having put on his rubber gloves before he even entered the house, he bent down over the body, looking for the best way to turn the dead man over.

Alex believed in putting a face on every case, every threat, that he could. It helped him process what was going on. In this case, since it involved the thwarted theft of high-end, expensive items, he was also curious about the dead man. Had he been the brains behind all this, or just a cog, taking orders? Not that the man's face could tell him that, but there might be other clues to be gotten from the would-be burglar.

As carefully as possible, Alex slowly turned the man over onto his back.

The moment he looked down at the dead man's face, everything around him faded into the background and vanished.

Alex recognized him.

Chapter 12

When she glanced over her shoulder to see what her partner was doing, Valri saw that he was crouching over the dead man. Instead of lying facedown the way he had been when they'd walked in, the suspected burglar was on his back. The CSI unit had already taken their pictures of the man and the immediate crime scene.

That meant that Brody had been the one to turn the body over.

As she watched Brody, it was hard for her to tell which of them was more still, her partner or the dead burglar.

Mumbling something about catching up with her

later, Valri left her sister and crossed over to where her partner was still crouching over the body.

He didn't seem to be aware of her presence. Even when she lightly touched his shoulder, it took him almost a minute to react to her.

That wasn't like him—at least as far as she knew, Valri amended.

"Hey, Brody, are you all right?" she asked him, concerned.

Alex roused himself and rose to his feet. Just because this was Eddie Brauer, a burglar who'd always been at the top of his game besides being a man his father had associated with on a fairly regular basis, didn't necessarily mean anything. After all, Brauer had pulled independent jobs before.

"Yeah, sure," Alex answered. "Why wouldn't I be?"

He sounded way too preoccupied for her taste, Valri thought. Something was definitely up.

"Well, for one thing, you look like you've just seen a ghost."

"No ghost," he answered a little too emphatically in her opinion. "Just another dead man." His tone was dismissive. "We need to talk to the homeowners," Alex said, moving past her.

"Kelly already took down their statements," she told him, hurrying to catch up to Brody. "She and her partner were first on the scene, thinking this was just a robbery," she added, explaining why the Robbery Division had been the first to be called in.

But Alex was determined to talk to the couple himself. "Maybe the husband remembers something after having his memory jostled," Alex said. "It wouldn't hurt to talk to both of them again."

"The wife's a basket case right now," she warned Brody.

It was a secondhand evaluation. She was merely repeating what Kelly had told her, but then there was no reason for Kelly to misrepresent anything. Familial harassment aside, she knew that her sister was a damn fine detective. Because of that, Valri took what her older sister said about the case as gospel.

"Maybe the wife'll do better talking to a fresh, sympathetic face," Alex told her.

"You?" she asked. *Sympathetic* was the last word she would have used to describe the current expression on Brody's face.

"Actually, I was thinking of you," he told her. "I'll talk to the husband."

Valri nodded, seeing no reason not to go along with what Brody was suggesting.

But I'm going to talk to you first opportunity I get, she promised herself. She wasn't convinced that Brody viewed the dead man as just another body. Something was not right there.

* * *

"Look at this," Clark Peters said to Alex as he took the homeowner aside and asked him to repeat his version of the events. Peters was referring to the hand he was holding out. "It's shaking," he said angrily, clearly distraught over what had just happened—as well as what *could* have happened had things gone just a little differently. "That could have been me lying there instead of him. I'm still shaking and I can't make myself stop." Not being able to control his own body was obviously really upsetting the homeowner.

"That's just your body reacting to what happened," Alex told the man. Peters was heavyset and appeared to have at least fifty pounds on the dead man in addition to being at least half a foot taller than Brauer. "It'll settle down in a little while," he assured Peters.

"So this is normal?" Peters asked, sounding as if he desperately wanted to be convinced.

"Perfectly," Alex assured him. "Now, why don't you tell me just what happened."

Peters obliged, ultimately giving him more than he wanted or needed. "No sooner did we get to our hotel room, than Judy and I get into this big fight." He looked over toward his wife, who was talking to the other detective. "The woman always has this lousy timing. She had to wait until I blow twelve thousand dollars on this vacation before she tells me she's 'unhappy' because I don't tell her little romantic things anymore. So I tell her when I look at her, I can't think of anything romantic to say."

Alex winced. Peters was obviously not a candidate for husband of the year. "Honesty is not always your best option, sir."

"Yeah, so I found out," Peters lamented. "The argument got out of hand, I canceled our stay at the hotel and we caught a flight back. Cost me a *bundle*," he declared, none too pleased.

"How long were you gone from home?" Alex asked, finally getting to something that was pertinent in his opinion.

"Less than twenty-four hours." The medical examiner and his assistant had placed the dead man into a black body bag and were now loading him onto a gurney. Peters watched the whole thing, as if to convince himself that it had actually happened. "Am I in trouble?" he asked nervously.

That had yet to be determined, Alex thought. He'd seen cases go absolutely haywire when unconventional evidence surfaced. Nothing was ever set in stone.

"Right now, sir, it appears to be an open-and-shut case of self-defense." He got down to the heart of the case. "Who knew you were going to be away?"

Peters thought for a moment. "Just a few people. Not that many. It *can't* be any one of them. I'd trust them with my life," he said dramatically.

"*How* did you tell them you were going away?" Alex asked.

Peters looked at him uncertainly. "How?" the homeowner repeated.

"That's what I said," Alex said, waiting.

"I emailed them," Peters told him. It was obvious by his tone that he didn't see what that had to do with anything. "I can give you their names if you want."

"That would be helpful," Alex replied congenially.

And probably unnecessary, he added silently. It was beginning to sound as if that surreal theory about a fake mobile cell tower collecting data from emails was right on the money. Hackers appeared to be everywhere and they were getting smarter by the minute.

It was far from a comforting thought.

This time when Valri approached him, Alex was ready for her and immediately asked, "Did you get anything from the wife?"

"Not really." Disappointed, Valri shook her head. "Just that she hadn't realized that her husband was so brave and I think she used the word *heroic*."

"Guess they won't be getting that divorce, then," Alex assumed.

"What?"

Brody reiterated what Latimore had initially told them. "The husband said they cut their vacation short because they had this huge fight, and from the sound of it, both of them were ready to call it quits and get a divorce."

"Now he's her hero," Valri said. "And all it took was killing a burglar."

"Yeah," he commented, more to himself than to her. "That's all."

After telling the couple to stay in town and to call if either of them could think of anything they'd forgotten to mention, Alex instructed them to do a thorough check of the house to see if anything beyond the painting that had been cut from its frame was missing.

Valri was dying to get to the shelter of his vehicle. The second they did and he got in behind the steering wheel, she asked Brody the question that had occurred to her when she saw him crouching over the dead man's body.

Brody knew the man. She was just positive that he did. The trick was going to be to get him to admit it. She decided on the direct approach rather than beating around the bush.

"You knew him, don't you?"

The question seemed to break apart the comfortable, speculative air within the inside of the vehicle.

Alex stopped pulling away from the curb. His hands tightened slightly on the steering wheel, but he managed to keep his voice at an even level as he flatly denied her assumption.

"No."

He wasn't fooling her. She'd seen the way Brody had looked at the dead man, seen him stiffen, then force himself to relax. Something didn't quite add up. She would *swear* to it.

"Your body language says otherwise," she informed him. Now that they were alone in the car and there was no one to overhear them, she could, she hoped, get some answers out of her partner.

"That's just your imagination running off with you," Alex scoffed. Everything about his manner told her that he refused to take her questioning seriously.

And refused to answer her questions, as well.

"No, it's not," she answered seriously, coming across a great deal more forcefully than he thought she was capable of sounding. "I'm fairly good at reading body language, and yours says that you know the man. How?" she asked him, then realized what he was probably thinking. "This goes no further," she assured him, waiting. After all, a man couldn't be held accountable for the people he might know in passing.

Alex remained silent.

Thinking.

Weighing things in his mind. He'd been carrying around the secret of his past—his upbringing—for a long time now. And rather than the load becoming lighter, it seemed to grow only heavier.

Maybe it *was* time he shared at least part of what bothered him with someone before he wound up suddenly imploding one day.

"Yeah, I know him. He's someone I met in passing a long time ago." He had a question of his own. "Just how did you get into reading body language?" Up until now, he'd always felt that he was pretty good at camouflaging his thoughts.

"I'm the youngest of seven," she told him matter-of-factly. "I did it in order to survive." She got back to the dead man. "Where did you meet him?"

He hadn't expected Cavanaugh to ask for details. He should have known better, he upbraided himself. "What?"

"The dead man, how did you happen to meet him?" she asked.

Alex thought of making something up, of lying to make things simpler. But lies, he knew, had a way of tripping a person up, and the whole point of going his own way was to stay clear of deception and to avoid living the same kind of secretive life that his father and his siblings led.

He had no choice but to clam up—or tell her the truth.

He went with the truth.

"I overheard him talking with my father one night a long time ago."

"So he's a friend of your father's?" she asked,

trying to read between the lines and piece things together.

"An associate of my father's," Alex corrected. "My father doesn't have friends." It occurred to Alex that he was referring to his father and the situation in the present tense, but it had been years since he'd seen or talked to anyone from his family. For all he knew, they were out of the business.

But he doubted it.

"What kind of associate?" she asked.

"A work associate," he answered, almost against his will. He was beginning to regret this. Maybe lying *would* have been easier.

"What kind of work does your father do?" Valri asked him.

He was *not* about to get into it.

"That's irrelevant," he told his partner. Okay, so he lied, but it was just a white lie, he argued silently. Under the circumstances, he figured he could be forgiven. "Listen, when we get back to the precinct, why don't you see if you can work your magic and match this guy up to a name. See if he's ever been arrested. Maybe he has a list of priors," he suggested, trying to distract her from asking him any more questions.

"You don't know his name?" Valri asked incredulously.

"I've got a name," he admitted. "But most likely it's an alias." He thought of the way Brauer had looked, lying there in a pool of his own blood. "People like that aren't overly concerned with giving out their real names." Pausing for a moment, Alex debated whether or not to mention anything else, or just let it ride. But he was beginning to see that his new partner was not the type to be content to merely coast along on the strength of her last name. She was a doer, someone who wanted to prove herself. If he kept quiet about Brauer, he had a feeling that she was going to dig up the details on her own.

He needed to get out in front of this before it dragged him down.

"I knew him as Uncle Eddie." When he was a kid, for simplicity's sake, his father referred to all of his "associates" as uncles. "Needless to say, he really wasn't my uncle."

This was hard for him, Valri realized. She could tell by his tone, his cadence. Talking about his family even in a cursory manner seemed to take a toll on him.

She could wait for the truth. It was more important to her to forge a relationship with her partner first. That might not happen if he felt she knew too much too soon. He might even resent her for it.

She cut bait.

"Someday, you're going to have to tell me about what happened," she told him casually.

Alex looked at her uncertainly. "What do you mean 'what happened'?"

"Between you and your family," she explained. "It's obvious that something had to go down in order for you to clam up like that every time there's the slightest mention of your family."

It wasn't so much that "something" had gone down as it was an entire way of life. His father prided himself on his skills to steal works of art without being caught or even, in some cases, having that theft detected for weeks, sometimes even years.

"That doesn't really have anything to do with this case," he told her.

"Maybe not," she allowed. "But it obviously has something to do with you and since it does—and you're my partner," she tossed in, "I'd really like to hear about it the second you're ready to talk."

She was letting him off the hook, he realized. For now. Was she being devious? Or simply nice? He wasn't sure yet.

"When I'm ready, you'll be the first to know," he promised.

"Hopefully you'll feel like sharing sometime *before* the Second Coming," she said wryly. She had no choice—if she wanted to build up a rapport—but to accept his promise at face value—and hope that it was true.

"At the very least, at the same time," he guaranteed, his tone indicating that he was at ease again. "Now, don't you have something you're supposed to be taking care of for the chief?" he prodded.

Valri's mouth dropped open. Damn, she'd totally forgotten about that. She'd become so completely caught up in both the current case and the mystery that was Detective Alex Brody, the fact that she was tasked with sending out invitations to Shamus Cavanaugh's wedding had totally slipped her mind.

"Oh God," she groaned, "I've got to get on that right away. Can you do the preliminary paperwork on the case so far?"

As the rookie member of the team, paperwork was supposed to be her job, but she couldn't do both, and if she waded through one before she took on the other, she'd wind up sleeping at her desk again.

"Consider it taken care of," he told her. "Don't give it another thought."

But I will give you another thought, Valri silently promised her partner. The second she finished notifying all these people about the wedding on Saturday. She glanced down at the list of names again.

Was it her imagination, or had the list somehow grown longer on its own?

Most likely, it was her imagination, she willingly granted. But it just seemed as if lately, everywhere she turned, there were Cavanaughs springing up out of the woodwork.

She got down to work.

By the time Alex walked into his one-bedroom garden-floor apartment, he felt as if his shift had gone a full eighteen hours. It hadn't, but in actuality, it had been pretty close. The paperwork had taken longer than he had anticipated, and he felt almost completely wiped out.

He also felt wound up.

As far as the latter went, he couldn't recall *ever* feeling this unsettled. Exhausted though he was, he had a feeling that getting to sleep tonight was going to be a problem.

Alex didn't turn on the light immediately when he let himself into his apartment.

Instead, he allowed himself to absorb the darkness, letting it enfold him in its shadowy arms as he did his best to will his body to relax. If he didn't unwind, at least to some degree, he could practically guarantee that he wasn't going to be able to sleep—which in turn meant that he would be totally dead on his feet all day tomorrow.

And if that happened, he was obviously not going to be at his best. That was when bad things occurred. This job needed people to be sharp and alert from the beginning of their shift to the end.

Sometimes longer.

Right at this moment, however, in addition to being wound up, he also felt like a tuning fork that had been struck and was vibrating, vacillating between two completely diverse states of mind.

The first involved attraction, deep, serious attraction.

The second revolved around the feeling that he should do everything in his power to avoid any and all entanglements with this woman.

The minute he opened the door, even just a crack, to admit any sort of feelings, however harmless and minor they might seem, he was a dead man.

As dead as Brauer—or whatever his real name was—had been on the floor of the Peterses' outlandishly oversize, overpriced house.

Ever since he'd "walked away" from the family business, he had tried to keep things as simple in his life as he could.

But it seemed that from the moment he had first caught this case, simplicity and his orderly life had gone straight out the window, apparently plummeting to their deaths.

Not only that, but things were getting more complicated every day.

And it wasn't just because there was a honey-blonde riding shotgun in his car—although she was part of it, he silently allowed. Maybe even a bigger part than he was willing to admit.

"You trying to save money on electricity by sitting in the dark, Alexander?"

A chill ran down his back. Several years had gone by since he'd heard that voice, but he would have recognized it even if decades had passed.

Finding the light switch on the wall behind him, Alex flipped it to the on position.

The overhead cam lights came on, flooding the immediate area with illumination.

Certainly more than enough light to show him that he'd been right.

Leland Philip Brody was sitting on his sofa in the living room.

"What are you doing here, Dad?"

Chapter 13

The man on the sofa allowed himself a small smile.

At first glance, he seemed more suited to being a preacher than to the vocation he had chosen for himself. The thin, trim athletic build was at odds with the full mane of silver-gray hair. It made pinpointing an age difficult, which was just the way Leland liked it.

He had spent the main portion of his life moving just under the radar. Recognition was a crutch for the insecure, for the people who never truly measured up but desperately wanted to be seen in that light. He preferred to concentrate on his craft, on attaining his target no matter how elusive and impossible it might initially seem.

Leland thought of what he did as an art form and he was an artist. His artistry was a gift that he gladly passed on to his progeny because they, along with his reputation, known to only a very small number of people, were all he would leave behind.

"Can't a father occasionally drop in on his son?" Leland asked innocently. "By my count, it's been a while."

Alex removed his service weapon and placed it where he always did, on the side table near the front door.

"It's been years," he corrected, "and I was under the impression that we were going to keep it that way."

Leland laughed quietly. "Ashamed of the old man, are we?"

Alex took a seat in the overstuffed chair facing the sofa—and his father.

"You'd be a little difficult to explain, but I'm not ashamed of you. I'd just rather that our paths wouldn't cross. That was the agreement, wasn't it?" It was the main reason he had worked his way up into Homicide—because he felt confident that he would never have to investigate his father. His father skillfully robbed people, he didn't kill them.

"Yes, it was. And it still is," Leland told him. Even after all this time, a hint of his Alabama childhood raised its head in the way he pronounced some of his words.

"And yet, here you are." Alex looked at his father, waiting for an explanation. This was *not* just a casual visit driven by nostalgia. That just wasn't his father's style.

"Like I said, I thought I'd just drop in on my youngest-born."

"You never do anything without a reason."

"Wanting to see how you were doing isn't enough?" Leland asked, amused.

Alex's eyes narrowed, his eyebrows forming a single dark line, underscoring his less than thrilled mood. "Not when it comes to you, no."

The laugh was dry, short. "You were always the brightest of the three. With a little work, you could have accomplished great things." It was as close to a lament regarding the past as Leland would allow himself.

"I'm doing just fine the way I am, thanks," Alex informed him curtly. "Now, why are you here? The truth, Dad, as strange a concept as that might be for you to contemplate."

The corners of Leland's thin mouth curved just the slightest bit. "I came to tell you in person that no one in the family was involved."

Alex watched his father for a long moment as he thought over the man's assurance. Leland Brody was a gifted, sought-after art forger as well as an art thief without equal. As far as he was concerned, his father had a great many character flaws, but he wasn't a liar.

"Involved in what?" Alex challenged.

Leland sighed impatiently. "Are we really going to draw this out?" he asked. When his son said nothing, Leland gave in and, for now, played along. He cited a few details. "Today's burglary. Today's *botched* burglary," he emphasized. "The one that got Brauer killed. I believe you caught the case."

He wasn't even going to ask his father how he knew. No matter what, his father *always* knew everything that was important to know.

Alex's eyes never left his father's. "You weren't in on it." It wasn't so much a question as an establishment of facts.

Leland inclined his head. "That's what I'm telling you."

"But you knew about it," Alex stated. He supposed if his father or Phil or Jenna had a police band radio, that would explain how he knew about the case.

"Not the details. Brauer and I have been out of touch for a number of years now. He'd gotten a little sloppy, took on jobs that he never would have thought twice about turning down back when we worked together."

All right, maybe his father didn't know details, but he had to know something. "What *do* you know about it?" Alex prodded.

Leland measured out each word as if he was doling out diamonds. "They get their information from email they collected via a signal coming off a mobile, virtual tower a couple of hackers created."

That his father knew this was astounding, but it wasn't anything new. "We already know that part."

"Bright boy," Leland said mockingly.

Alex ignored the comment. Since his father obviously knew something about the robbery, he intended to get as much out of him as he could.

"Who set up the virtual tower and collected the data? There has to be more than just Brauer in on this."

"There's no arguing that," his father agreed. "Brauer's specialty was overriding security systems—man was a master—not any of that other stuff," Leland confirmed.

"So who was he working with or for?" Alex asked. Someone had to have come up with the idea and then the means to gather the information.

Leland spread his hands. "I don't have any names, but word on the street has it that it was one of those gamers-turned-hacker."

The description fit the first dead man. Alex shook his head. "Gotta do better than that, Dad. Rogers wouldn't have offed himself."

A smug look filtered through Leland's steel-blue eyes. "I'm not talking about Rogers. The brains of his operation is someone else. That's who Brauer approached to facilitate the burglaries. Supposedly it was a so-called friend of Rogers's and they worked together on the 'project.'" Leland laughed shortly. There was no humor in the sound, just a pervading sense of emptiness. "Friends like that—you know the rest."

"Yeah, I know the rest," Alex murmured, his mind racing. A friend of Rogers's turned executioner. Whom had he overlooked? "Anything else?" he asked his father.

Leland rose to his feet, as did Alex. He never took his eyes off his father. Father or not, Leland Brody wasn't a man you let your guard down around. His end game was always hidden until the very last second, and Alex didn't care for surprises.

"No," Leland said, crossing over to the door. "I've said what I came to say. Just didn't want you to think I reneged on our agreement." Resting his hand on the doorknob, he paused for a moment to really look at his son. "You doing all right, Alexander?"

It depended on the definition of "all right." If "all right" wasn't too demanding, then he was fine. "I can't complain."

"No, you were never one to do that," Leland recalled. "That's why the others always thought you were your mother's favorite." Still at the door, he appeared to be debating saying something further before he left. Alex saw just the slightest shrug of his shoulder before his father said, "Maybe if she had lived, things would have been different."

"Maybe," Alex allowed. His mother had always been the peacemaker. She knew she had married an art thief, but she managed to get him to attempt to lead a normal, civilian life. He did it for her until he couldn't do it any longer. His mother accepted that.

Had she lived, Alex knew that his break from the family would have been that much harder for him, but he would have had to do it in order to survive. After his mother had died, he felt more estranged from the others than ever. Going his own way just seemed like the logical thing for him to do.

His father was lingering too long. "Is there something else?" Alex asked.

Rather than answer one way or another, his father merely said, "Take care of yourself, Alexander."

"You, too, Dad."

Leland closed the door behind him, but his presence would take longer to dissipate. As would the emotions that had been stirred by the man's unexpected visit.

Taking out a small notepad that had seen many better days, Alex made notes to himself about his father's impromptu appearance.

"I want to take another run at Jason Bigelow," Alex said to his partner the following morning. It was the first thing out of his mouth the moment he walked in.

Valri was already in the squad room and at her desk, working on something. From the looks of it, she'd been there awhile. There was no steam rising from her coffee mug, which meant that the liquid in it was cold. Since she brought it to her desk before she sat down, that meant she'd been here for a while.

"Why?" She didn't think of it as extra work, but she wanted to know his reasoning. If they were going to be working together—and it was beginning to look that way—they had to get in sync with each other, know how the other thought and reacted to things. The information was half gleaned from everyday interaction and half from observing the other party in action.

"Let's just call it a hunch," Alex told her evasively.

But she wanted more than that. He didn't strike her as someone who was careless, tossing everything against the wall to see what stuck.

"A hunch based on what?"

She asked too many questions, he thought irritably. He had no intention of saying his father had paid him a visit last night and gave him information. That would be opening up a very messy can of worms.

"Hunches don't have to be based on anything," he told her.

"Yeah, they do," she contradicted. "Was there

something that jumped out at you in your report that hadn't occurred to you before?"

Okay, he'd go with that, Alex thought. "I just went over the entire interview with Bigelow and he just didn't seem to be completely forthcoming with us." He could see that she wasn't being convinced, so he tried another tactic. "He wasn't afraid enough."

Confused, she stared at Alex. "Come again?"

"Think back," he instructed. "Wills was scared to death of the person who killed Rogers."

"And with good reason. The guy killed Wills," she reminded him.

"That's my point. There's this history of violence with our mystery hacker. Bigelow claimed he saw the guy, yet he wasn't worried about that guy coming back to permanently silence him the way he had Rogers. That doesn't add up for me."

Valri thought it over for a moment and played devil's advocate. "It could just be that Bigelow wasn't smart enough to think it through and realize how much danger he was in."

She wrinkled her nose when she was working on a problem in her head. It added a degree of adorable to the whole thing, something he knew she'd be appalled about if he so much as mentioned it to her.

What had gotten into him? Alex silently demanded. They were working a murder case. That was supposed to take precedence over everything.

"Maybe," he agreed without too much conviction. "But I still want to question him again."

She saved her work on the laptop and rose. "Okay, let's do it," she said gamely. "Let's go find our 'nerves of steel' gamer."

"You're really going to be embarrassed when I turn out to be right," he told her.

"More like really astonished," she fired back, managing to keep a straight face.

When they arrived at the guesthouse where Bigelow lived on his mother's property, no lights were on in the two-room structure.

When no one answered the door after Alex had rung the bell three times, he let himself and Cavanaugh in the old-fashioned way.

He quickly picked the lock.

"That was no challenge at all," he murmured. "The guy has to get a better lock than that."

"Maybe he thinks nobody's going to bother breaking into a gamer's home," she said, watching Alex make quick work with the lock. Then her admiration got the better of her. "You have to teach me that, someday," she said enviously.

"Someday," he agreed. Acutely aware of his surroundings, he slowly turned the doorknob and let himself and Valri into the house.

Service weapon poised, he held on to it with both hands as he visually swept the area.

Valri was right behind him.

All the gaming equipment was just where it had been when they came here the other day. There was only one thing missing: Bigelow. The gamer who had given them the description of the man who had paid Rogers to come up with a way to hack into a cell phone tower to create a duplicate was nowhere in sight.

From all appearances, the two-room guesthouse was empty.

"He's not here," Bigelow's mother informed them.

Curious to see what was going on, she had followed the two detectives to her son's living quarters. She stood in the guesthouse doorway now, her short, robust frame filling the area completely.

"Where is he?" Alex asked.

Shoulders that were better suited to a football guard rose and fell dismissively. "Damned if I know. You think he tells me anything? I'm good enough to cook for him and toss his dirty laundry into the washer, but not good enough to be told any of his plans," she grumbled. "*Then* he's this adult who comes and goes as he pleases."

Ethel Bigelow glanced from Alex to his partner. "Do yourselves a favor, you two. Don't have kids. Nothing but regret and trouble from the minute they're born."

The woman looked as if she was just getting wound up to talk. He had a feeling they wouldn't learn anything except how thankless it was to be a mother. It was time to leave.

"We'll keep that in mind, ma'am. And if you hear from him, give us a call," Alex requested, handing her one of his cards. "We just need to ask him a few more questions."

The woman sneered at them, priding herself on not being taken in for a moment. "Is that why you had your guns out? To ask my son questions?"

"No, ma'am, that's strictly for precaution in case there was someone in the house with your son who had a gun on him. We've been taught not to take any unnecessary chances," Valri told the woman, deliberately assuming a calm, soothing cadence in order to keep the woman from becoming agitated.

Not that she would have blamed her. If she had a child who was missing, life would have come to a grinding halt until that child was safely back in her arms.

Mrs. Bigelow nodded. "Yeah, I guess that makes sense. Some of the people that my son hangs out with don't exactly look like they're marching off to Sunday school, if you get my drift. Can't tell him anything, though. He knows best," she said with complete disgust.

"Kids can be ungrateful," Valri commiserated. "Don't forget to call if you think of something else," she reminded the woman.

* * *

"So back to the drawing board?" she asked Alex when they got into his car several minutes later.

"Not entirely," he told her. "I'm going to have Mara work up a sketch of Bigelow and start circulating that. Maybe we'll get lucky and someone's seen him."

"You really think he has something to do with this, don't you?"

"Yes, I do," Alex affirmed as he drove to one of the city's main thoroughfares, Culver Drive. And then a thought occurred to him. He spared her a quick glance. "Why, you don't?"

"I haven't made up my mind yet—but I can see why it would be a definite possibility," she agreed. "On a different note, are you coming?"

That wasn't a different note, it was a completely different melody, he thought. Preoccupied with the theory his father had handed him, she had caught him off guard with her question.

"Coming to what?" he asked.

"To the wedding," Valri said patiently. "You got your invitation, I know you did."

"Oh, right. That." Alex shook his head. He didn't have time for that. "I don't do weddings."

Now there was a dumb excuse, she couldn't help thinking.

"No one's asking you to get married, just to show up and watch the ceremony. Most of the department's coming," she added. "You don't want to be the one no-show."

"And if it's going to be that crowded, how would anyone notice?" he asked.

"I would notice," she told him. "C'mon, Brody," she coaxed. "It'll be fun. I promise."

He let a silver sports car get ahead of him. "You can't promise that."

"Oh, yes I can," she told him, her eyes shining as she said it.

He had to admit it made him very curious. What did she have in mind?

It didn't matter what her intentions were, he argued with himself. He needed to keep her at arm's length at all times. He couldn't allow any so-called feelings to even remotely poke through. He had his career to think of.

"If I have the time, I'll come," he told her, thinking that would be enough to put her off. "Now let's get Bigelow's description to Mara so she can work up that sketch."

"How about if we just circulate his picture instead?" Valri suggested.

He slanted a quizzical glance at her. She was talking as if she had a photo to work with. "You have his picture?" he questioned, surprised. "Where did you get it?" he asked. "Facebook?"

"Actually, I have it on my phone." She pulled up the app where her photographs were stored and scrolled to the collection of photographs she'd taken at the last gamers' convention. "Here," she declared, holding up her phone so that Brody could see, "this is a good one to use."

"When did you get that?" he asked. Had she had that all along? Just how close was she to Bigelow, anyway?

"Last year, at the big gaming convention in Las Vegas," she told him.

Something wasn't adding up. "I thought you said that gaming was in your past."

"Every now and then, I get nostalgic," she admitted with a careless shrug. "I like to keep my hand in, see if I've still got what it takes to make a competent showing. The competition keeps me sharp," she told him.

"You know, that innocent-little-girl look of yours is pretty damn deceptive—but you can only play that card a limited amount of times."

She grinned at him. "I'll take that as a compliment," she told Alex, then added, "Thank you—but that still doesn't get you off the hook. You're still coming to the wedding."

"Why is it so important to you that I show up?" he asked. Why should it matter whether or not he came?

"Because I want you to experience what it's like to have a family around you, people who care," she emphasized.

"One little problem with that. They're your family," he pointed out. "Not mine."

"You're wrong there," she told him. "It's yours, too."

"And just how do you figure that?" he asked. This was going to be good, he anticipated. He was beginning to think that Valri would have made one hell of a grifter.

"Uncle Andrew considers every single member of the police force to be 'family.' Family isn't just about DNA or biology anymore," she argued. "Family is a mind-set, a way of viewing people you care about, people whom you wish well. People who matter in your day-to-day life."

Alex sighed. He wasn't going to have any peace until he went along with her plans to attend the wedding, he knew that. Or at least *say* that he was going to attend.

"Did you ever consider transferring to the department's public relations section?" he asked her, both irritated and amused. "You'd be a natural at it."

"I'd much rather gather converts one at a time," Valri told him with a wide, guileless grin. "C'mon, let's get copies of this photograph printed up and into circulation. Meanwhile, I've got a few people to call. Maybe someone on the circuit has seen him."

"The circuit?" he asked, not sure what she was referring to.

"The gaming circuit. A lot of really good gamers make their living going from one competition to another. Some are online, others require the players be seated within sight of one another."

"Of course they do," he murmured under his breath. This was a whole way of life he hadn't known existed. And now that he did, it still didn't matter to him—beyond closing this case, hopefully sometime before the turn of the next century.

Chapter 14

After two days of intensified searching, they were still nowhere. It was as if Jason Bigelow had just vanished into thin air.

Valri had come up with a list of people who associated with the gamer, either in person or, more likely, online during one of the tournaments.

Everyone she and Alex questioned told them the same thing: The person hadn't heard from Bigelow since the day after the so-called "King" had been killed.

"Is it me, or is every avenue we try bringing us to another dead end?" Alex asked as he and Valri wearily got back into his car.

"Definitely not you," Valri assured him, sitting in the passenger seat. She buckled up out of habit without even being aware of it. Blowing out a breath, she shook her head.

"What?" Alex asked. At this point, he was grasping at straws, but there had to be a lead here somewhere. Sometimes, the most offhanded comment triggered things and made them fall into place.

"I was just thinking, so much for Bigelow being concerned about his mother's welfare," she said, referring to what the gamer had said the first time they'd questioned him. He'd expressed concern that if something happened to him, there would be no one to look after his mother.

It was Alex's turn to laugh dismissively. "From what I saw, his mother was the one taking care of him."

"No argument," she agreed. "Taking care of Number One is his only concern." She thought a moment as Alex pulled into the main flow of traffic. "He's either dead—or he's the brains behind this whole thing."

"That's a hell of a leap," Alex commented. He kept to himself the fact that he had already begun to lean toward the second possibility. But since that late-night visit from his father, it was beginning to look more and more as if Rogers was the other hacker Brauer had come to with his proposition.

"Maybe not so much," Valri theorized. "Remember my sister Kelly? The one where the burglar was killed by Clark Peters, the home owner?" she added to help him make the connection. "She told me that the rash of burglaries has stopped."

He supposed that the crew—if there *was* a crew—could be lying low for a while. There was also another theory. "Could it have been that small an operation, just Rogers, Brauer and the third hacker?"

She was quickly learning that when it came to criminals, *anything* was possible.

"Either that, or the rest of the 'gang' is lying low for a while," she said, giving voice to what he'd been thinking. It surprised Alex that he liked that they were in sync this way. "In any case, it's Friday afternoon and we've done all we can for the moment until something else comes up. The weekend's just about here and I'm not going to think about dead hackers, runaway gamers and art heists right now. We've got a wedding to attend tomorrow," she told him brightly.

He'd really been hoping she wouldn't bring that up again. He supposed he should have known better. "About that—"

Valri headed him off. "If you're going to say anything other than you're coming, I don't want to hear it," she told him.

He sighed. "This stubborn streak you keep displaying, is it just unique to you or is it a trait that all the Cavanaughs share?"

Her smile was wide and unnervingly innocent. "Come to the wedding and find out."

Alex had to laugh. "You really just don't give up, do you?"

Valri lifted her chin just a little bit as she answered, "Never."

That was the truest thing she'd said to him so far, Alex thought.

His plan was to ignore whoever was on the other side of his door the next morning, even though they were knocking loud enough to wake up the dead. Alex knew that his unexpected would-be visitor wasn't his father because after one failed attempt to gain entry into the apartment via the normal route, Leland Brody would have let himself in with his skeleton key.

Most likely, whoever was banging on his door was either Valri or another member of her family, dispatched to bring him to the wedding whether he wanted to go or not.

"No" was obviously not part of the Cavanaugh vocabulary.

So not answering was the way he was going to go.

Until the door suddenly opened on its own.

The next second, Valri hurried in on what appeared to be five-inch heels.

"I'm a pretty quick study," she told him in response to the stunned expression on his face. "I watched you break into Bigelow's house, remember?"

He made some sort of sound, intended to be taken as agreement. Or at any rate, he thought he made an agreeable noise. However, the stunned expression on his face had nothing to do with her mastering the art of breaking and entering and everything to do with the woman in the shimmery, sky-blue dress standing inside his apartment. She looked as if she'd ridden in on the latest sunbeam.

"Valri?" he asked uncertainly.

Alex was aware enough to know that if he used her surname the way he usually did, considering the event that was happening today, it wasn't going to narrow things down at all. The Cavanaughs were one hell of an oversize family if ever there was one.

"Of course it's me," she answered, frowning at him. "Who were you expecting?"

"Not you," he said, unable to draw his eyes away. "Not like that, at any rate," he added, close to speechless.

This was his partner? The woman he rode with these past couple of weeks looked like the poster girl for a beach bunny, or at the very least, a cheerleader who spent her entire summers at the beach.

What he was looking at right now was a woman who could melt away his very knees. Her dress was all glitter and dreams and not much else. It was clinging to her curves and ending far above her knees. The brilliant blue color brought out her eyes even more than usual.

So much so that he felt as if someone had punched him in the gut, stealing his very breath away.

Her hair, always pulled back in a ponytail or clipped back and up, out of her way, was free now, flowing just below her shoulders like a blanket of golden sunbeams.

"You're not even dressed," she complained.

Instead of answering, or making some sort of an excuse, he continued standing there, his eyes never leaving her.

Finally, Valri felt she had to say something. "You're staring at me."

"Uh-huh. Did you always clean up this well?" he asked her.

Valri frowned. "Very funny. Now get in there and get dressed," she ordered, pointing to the rear of his apartment, where she assumed his bedroom was located.

Alex looked down at his pullover and torn jeans. "I am dressed," he told her.

"Get dressed *better*," she emphasized. "You do own a suitable jacket to wear to a wedding, don't you?" she asked, then warned, "Think carefully. Because if the answer is no, I can call one of my brothers to drop one off for you."

"I've got a jacket," he told her, sounding none too happy. The last thing he wanted was to be wearing a loaner jacket provided by one of her brothers. He didn't want to get sucked into the Cavanaugh vortex if he could possibly help it.

The family had a habit of absorbing people, bringing them into the fold. Alex felt he was much too independent for that.

"And a tie? Dress pants, nice shirt?" she quizzed hopefully.

He made no answer. Instead, he went into the bedroom.

She listened, but didn't hear the bedroom door closing. If he was putting on other clothes, wouldn't he have shut the door?

"Are you changing?" she called out.

"Why, you want to come in here and supervise?" he asked.

"I'll leave you on your honor," she told him.

She assumed that he was going to need a few minutes to get dressed, so she busied herself by looking around. As she moved through the living room, she was struck by the lack of anything that would have provided a personal touch to the apartment.

There were no photographs, no books to indicate what he favored reading, no sports paraphernalia haphazardly dropped on the floor as he hurried to get ready for work, or make an appointment.

Nothing was out of its place.

There was also nothing to indicate that anyone

actually *lived* here. "Did you just move in here?" she asked, raising her voice so he could hear her.

"No," Alex answered, walking out of the bedroom. "Why?"

He cleaned up well, Valri couldn't help thinking. *Very* well. She'd acknowledged from the first moment she'd met him that he was one good-looking man, but seeing him in a suit just somehow seemed to emphasize that.

Rousing herself, she said, "Because I don't see anything personal of yours here. No pictures, no books or CDs. Nothing that says 'Alex Brody lives here.'"

"It doesn't have to. I'm here. That's personal enough," he told her. "So, do I pass your inspection?" he asked mockingly.

Her eyes met his, conveying a great deal more than she was willing to say out loud yet.

"More than pass," she assured him. "I think maybe I should bring my weapon."

That came out of left field, Alex thought. He wasn't sure he understood her meaning. "Why?"

"To keep some of the more enthusiastic women from grabbing you and running off with you tucked under their arm."

Alex could only laugh. "I had no idea you had this flair for dramatic exaggeration."

Her smile turned into an appealing grin. "Neither did I, Brody."

* * *

Possibly because of his unorthodox upbringing, Alex wasn't a man who was easily impressed or overwhelmed. But he had to admit that the sight of so many police personnel gathered together other than outside of an auditorium briefing momentarily took his breath away.

"Takes your breath away, doesn't it?" Valri asked, leaning in so that only he could hear her.

She'd used the exact same description that had occurred to him in his head, Alex realized. Not only that, but at the same time she'd managed to make his knees a shade weaker because he had simultaneously experienced the arousing feel of her breath along the side of his face and neck as she whispered. And that in turn mingled with the scent of her light, enticing perfume.

If he didn't know better, he would have said that his head was spinning. But that sort of a reaction was for adolescents—or someone who had been drugged. And he was neither—or at least, not the first.

"I grew up with a large family by modern standards, but the first time I attended one of Uncle Andrew's little parties, I felt pretty stunned and not a little disoriented."

"They should be wearing name tags," he quipped. He heard her laugh and the sound just wound itself into his belly, causing strange things to happen in response. He was going to have to watch himself. If he was this way without having anything to drink, the toll would really be high once he started.

"That's what I said the first time, too. Initially, it would really make things easier," she agreed. "But I've gotten pretty good at learning names. Consider me your guide through the land of Cavanaugh— for today," she told him.

He could have sworn that her eyes were shining as she spoke to him.

It amazed him how easily Valri slipped her arm through his, as if they had been in this sort of an easygoing relationship for a long time instead of being partnered because of the job and together for only a couple of weeks.

"You wait here," Valri requested. "I'll go get us a couple of beers."

"Forgive me if my etiquette is a little rusty. I don't get much of a chance to socialize lately, but shouldn't I be the one getting a beer for you?"

"I don't stand on ceremony, you know that. Besides," she said just before she left, "if I leave you here in the center of this throng, chances are I'll find you here—as long as you don't wander off."

"I'll be right here," he assured her as he watched Valri walk away.

"So how's it going?" a deep male voice behind him asked not thirty seconds later.

The question was directed at him, Alex realized when he turned around.

Brian Cavanaugh looked distinguished, but light-years away from the man who had the fate of the world on his shoulders. The man was nursing a beer, but his attention was unwaveringly aimed at him, to the exclusion of everyone else there.

"We've hit a stalemate in the investigation," Alex replied, being honest.

"You'll work through it," Brian replied as if he had the utmost faith in him as well as in his grand-niece. "But I wasn't asking you about that. I was asking about the two of you working together. How's *that* going? Any major problems?"

"Well, she's really stubborn," Alex felt obligated to mention.

Brian laughed. "That's a Cavanaugh thing, I'm afraid. And it's twice as pronounced in the Cavanaugh women as it is in the Cavanaugh men. But, properly channeled, it can work to your advantage," he told the younger man with a wink.

The chief had to be pulling his leg, Alex thought. Right?

As if reading his mind, Brian put his free arm around his back and said, "Relax, boy. This is a party. My father has found someone who hasn't heard all his stories yet and will actually listen to him tell them. In my book, that alone is a reason for celebration. That she's willing to marry him as well is a huge bonus." He glanced at his watch. "You've just got enough time to get a drink. The ceremony's going to start in a few minutes." He dropped his hand to his side. "Andrew has everything timed down to the minute. He always has. I suppose that there's no other way to run things with a family that's this big."

As if on cue, Valri returned, offering Alex his choice of beers. After he picked one, Valri took a long, healthy drink of hers, then lowered the bottle.

"Looks like we made it just in time," she said, slanting a quick glance in his direction. "Let's go pick out a good place to stand," she coaxed. "They're holding the wedding outside," she explained. "It's the only place that could accommodate everyone. Otherwise, someone would get left out."

He could see that. What astonished him, once he was outside, was that they all fit out here. At first glance, he would have said that it was impossible, dispite the size of the yard. This was one huge group. But then he recalled what the chief had said about Cavanaughs all being stubborn.

"All these people..." Alex looked around at the people gathered together. More kept arriving. It was, in a word, overwhelming. "Are they really your family?"

"Every last one of them—and some friends thrown in for good measure," she reminded him. "Every Cavanaugh who isn't married or spoken for was allowed to bring a friend," she explained. "And of course there are a few friends here, but a lot of the people Shamus once knew have either moved away, or moved on," she said significantly, preferring the euphemism to the cold hard facts.

"And there also wasn't time to notify everyone, considering that the groom only gave us four days' notice. A lot of people, retired or not, can't just re-arrange their lives and hop a plane or drive like crazy to get here. If Shamus and Lucy were doing this in Florida, there wouldn't be nearly this many people attending. But then, if this was Florida, he would never have met Lucy because she lived here, with her granddaughter and great-granddaughter."

He wasn't following her. "Why would this be tak-ing place in Florida?"

"That's where Shamus went to live when he first retired. But after the active life he'd led—being a police chief before Andrew took on the role—being retired with an endless amount of time on his hands drove him crazy. So one night he just walked out the front door of the retirement home and kept on going. He eventually flagged down a car that took him to the bus station. From there he just kept con-necting with different buses until he finally arrived in Southern California and came back here."

"That takes guts," Alex said with admiration. "The whole lot of them, they're crusty," he assessed.

There was pride in her smile. "That they are,"

she agreed. "Every last one of them. Every last one of us," she corrected.

Drawing him into the backyard as far as she could, Valri left him standing there as she scouted out a place that suited her purposes. It had a clear view of the happy couple as well as allowed them to see other couples who had come to attend the wedding.

Satisfied, Valri went to get Alex. "I found a perfect place," she told him. Taking his hand, she quickly retraced her steps in order to claim the spot before someone else took it.

She got back just in time. One of her cousins looked to be headed for the exact same spot. But since she and Brody had reached it first, her cousin fell back and searched for another spot.

Safe. Valri let go of the breath she'd been holding the entire time. From here, they could see the bride's entire march down the aisle as well as watch the vows being exchanged.

"This is good," she pronounced.

"Yes, it is," he agreed.

Glancing at him, she noticed that he didn't appear to be referring to the spot she'd selected for them. Instead, he was looking directly at her.

A warmth spread through her a beat before the wedding march began playing.

Focus, Val, focus, she ordered herself. This was no time to allow herself to drift inward. This was a very special occasion and it deserved her full attention. It wasn't every day that she got to witness a storybook beginning for a couple as seasoned in years as her great-granduncle Shamus and Lucy, a great-grandmother.

"Who's the little girl?" Alex asked, whispering the question in her ear.

Another warm shiver shimmied up and down her spine, spreading a blanket of heat everywhere. "That's Lucy's great-granddaughter and my brother's future stepdaughter."

"God, you really can't tell the players without a scorecard, can you?" Alex murmured.

She knew just how he felt. She'd been part of this extended family for over a year now and she was just beginning to have confidence in her ability to tell everyone apart. "Don't worry, it takes time, but it'll come easier with each encounter."

"You say that as if that's going to be a regular thing," he observed.

She spared him a grin before turning back to watch the bride walking down the aisle on her brother Duncan's arm. "They have a lot of weddings and birthday parties," she told him just as Lucy, dressed in a long cream-colored lacy wedding gown, stopped before the priest waiting for them at the altar that had been lovingly constructed by some of the handier Cavanaughs.

Shamus, Valri observed, was positively beaming when his bride came to stand by him.

"I guess it's never too late to find love," she heard Alex comment.

"I guess not," she whispered back.

And then everyone fell silent as Shamus and Lucy, looking into each other's eyes, took the vows that would forever bind them to one another.

Chapter 15

"Okay, I'll admit it," Alex said when, hours later, they finally left the reception and Valri was driving him back to his apartment. A bright full moon illuminated their way.

"Admit what?" Valri asked, curious.

"That you Cavanaughs really do know how to throw one hell of a party."

Although, looking back now, he had to admit that he resisted it, he had felt welcomed right from the start. More important than that, he hadn't felt like the outsider. A sense of belonging just naturally materialized out of nowhere, easily slipping over him without his even taking note of it. Apparently, the Cavanaughs had that effect on people.

"Is that your offhanded way of saying that you had a good time?" Valri asked, trying to coax the words out of him.

Alex laughed to himself. Some things were harder to admit because he thought if he said anything, he'd forfeit the very thing he was praising. Superstition had been a way of life in his family before he was old enough to realize what a big role it played in that world.

"Yeah, I guess it is."

This was getting good, Valri thought, really pleased on behalf of her family...and maybe a little for herself.

"And you're glad I made you go to the wedding?"

"'Glad' is stretching it a little," Alex hedged. He noticed the look she shot him, as if she could see right into his mind and knew what he was thinking. "Okay, okay, yes, I'm glad. Satisfied?"

Valri grinned. "I'm getting there."

She made a right at the end of the block, then an immediate sharp left to enter his apartment complex. The path to his ground-floor apartment was a winding one. Guest parking proved to be rather full and it took her a few minutes to find a space. She squeezed her small, reliable two-door between a pickup that was so new it still didn't have license plates and a gold Cadillac Escalade SUV with a dimpled bumper that had *not* originally come with the vehicle.

"Well, here you are, safe and sound, back in your own lair," she announced, turning off her engine.

"Door-to-door service, it doesn't get any better than that," Alex quipped. He opened the passenger door and was about to get out when he noticed that she hadn't opened her door yet.

Even though he knew it would be best if he just wrapped up the night right here, right now, and let her go home, Alex heard himself asking, "Would you like to come in for a little while?"

"What, you haven't had more than your fill of Cavanaughs?" she deadpanned. A second later, the corners of her mouth curved in amusement.

"Oddly enough, no, I haven't."

"Well, who could possibly resist a line like that?" she asked. "Not me."

Opening the door on her side, Valri got out. Pressing the button on her key, she sent both car locks into hiding at the same time.

Alex waited until she was beside him before he led the way to his apartment. As she matched him step for step, all he could think of was that she seemed petite and graceful. No one looking at her would have ever suspected she was proficient enough in martial arts to send the average man falling to his knees in an instant, most likely whimpering.

This woman would never allow herself to be a damsel in distress, he mused. Any fantasies he might have evolved in his head would have to remain just that: fantasies.

"Are all the Cavanaugh parties like that?" he asked. When she raised a quizzical eyebrow, obviously waiting for a clearer question, he finally said, "So…enthusiastic," for lack of a better descriptive word to fit the behavior he'd witnessed.

She nodded. "More or less, yes. At least, the ones I've attended were like that. Sometimes the group is a little smaller, but I don't think I've ever seen a larger one than the one that was there today. Just about *everyone* showed up to see the chief of Ds' father get married."

"What do you think the odds are that there were any cops left patrolling Aurora?" he joked.

"Pretty good, actually. Four or five cops at least," she estimated with a straight face.

He fished his key out of his pocket and put it into the lock.

"I've got some beer and a couple of bottles of root beer in the refrigerator if you like," he offered her. Opening his door, he stepped to one side, his indication clear.

"What else do you have?" Valri asked, walking into his apartment in front of him.

She heard the door close behind them. Why was that sound so sensual, so compelling? She turned to face him and just like that, she felt her pulse rate increasing. It was as if everything within her had been waiting just for this moment.

The perfect storm.

"What I have is a really strong desire to do this," Alex answered, his voice almost whisper quiet.

The next moment, he had framed her face with his hands and kissed her.

He was as surprised as she probably was by the amount of passion that suddenly surfaced.

It infused itself into what, at its inception, was supposed to have been a simple kiss. A kiss whose life expectancy should have been as quick as a heartbeat. Instead, it wasn't quick, it was beating hard, like a drumroll that refused to end.

Her mouth tasted sweeter than he'd ever thought anything could. Sweeter and intoxicatingly addicting.

That part he hadn't counted on. Hadn't thought through.

Hadn't thought possible.

Like the classic love song said, a kiss was just a kiss—but not in this case. In this case, a kiss—*their* kiss—didn't feel like just a kiss.

It felt like a beginning.

A beginning that he desperately wanted to see through to the end. But despite what he *wanted*, Alex knew he couldn't follow this to its conclusion, for a number of reasons. The most glaring of which was that they were partners and they were detectives.

"Oh wow," Alex murmured when he finally forced himself to end the kiss and back away.

"My feelings exactly." She looked at him for a long moment. The warm glow within her grew. "I had no idea that was choice number three right after the beer and root beer. If I had, I might have stopped by here sooner," she told Alex.

"I'm sorry, I didn't mean to do that."

"Funny, I could have sworn that you did." Valri made no attempt to move away.

This wasn't easy for him, but he forced the words out. "I think you'd better go before we wind up doing something we'll regret."

Her eyes were smiling at him as she said, "Unless you're planning on committing us to participate in some awful reality program that involves taking on and wrestling a bunch of seminaked, scruffy people on an island, regret is not on the agenda."

Didn't she understand he was trying to get her to leave for her own good? He certainly wasn't doing this for himself.

Alex tried again, telling her honestly, "Look, I want to kiss you again."

"Okay." Valri laced her arms around his neck. "I'm fine with that."

His body was heating at a prodigious rate. With more willpower than he usually needed to summon, he removed Valri's arms from across his shoulders. Holding on to her hands, he told her honestly, "But if I do, if I kiss you, it's not going to stop there."

"So far I'm not hearing a problem," she told him, her voice low and sexy. The very sound of it was swiftly undoing him.

He tried again, doing his best to make Valri understand why this *couldn't* be allowed to happen between them.

"Look, we're partners. If we cross the line tonight, we're going to have to tell Latimore and he'll assign us to different partners. And I don't want a different partner," he stressed. "I want you."

He had no idea how much that meant to her. Considering the way he had looked at her when they first met and the chief had paired them up, Valri felt as if she had just succeeded in getting the brass ring.

"It's none of Latimore's business what we're doing here tonight—or any other night," Valri stressed. "The only reason to stop is if *we* don't want this to happen. And I don't know about you, Brody, but I certainly vote yes."

He wasn't doing this for himself. He was doing it for her, for her safety.

"You still don't understand, do you? If this happens tonight, it'll change everything." He looked deep into her eyes, searching for a glimmer of understanding. "It'll change the way we operate."

Her brow furrowed slightly. "I'm afraid you're

going to have to explain that to me because I'm not following you."

"If my feelings about you change, if I'm worried about your safety while we're pursuing someone, that'll take away my edge. And I won't be able to do my job as well as I should."

"Does that mean you don't normally concern yourself about your partner's safety?" Valri challenged.

"Yes, of course I do." He blew out a frustrated breath. "You're twisting things."

"No," she contradicted. "I'm clarifying things. As partners, we have each other's back." Her arms slipped back up around his neck. "We're there for each other no matter what." She tried to put it into perspective for him. "If, instead of who I am, I was a two-hundred-and-fifty-pound guy nicknamed Moose, you'd still have my back, still come to my rescue if I was in danger, wouldn't you?"

"Well, yes, sure, but—"

She glossed right over the last word. "So the situation—and the way you react—is not going to be any different from what it would be if we get to know each other in the biblical sense or not."

Alex gave up trying to remove her arms from his neck. It just wasn't in him to fight his own feelings *and* her. Not when he wanted her so badly.

"You're wasted as a cop, you know that, right?"

Alex asked her. "You should be in the DA's office, having your way with words."

But Valri shook her head, disagreeing with his assessment. "I'm exactly where I'm supposed to be." She moved in even closer to him. "Now, stop talking and kiss me."

"Yes, ma'am," he murmured.

Valri pulled back her head just for a moment. "You call me 'ma'am' again," she warned, "and your mouth'll be too bruised to kiss anything."

He wasn't quite sure if she was serious or kidding. He was about to say as much when Valri suddenly rose up on her toes and very effectively sealed her mouth to his.

Sealed his fate as well because his immediate future was suddenly clear as crystal.

He abandoned the safeguards he'd so carefully constructed around his feelings, barriers that were supposed to keep him safe from accidentally getting involved with a woman who was definitely *not* one-night-stand material. He had immediately sensed that about Valri the moment he'd met her.

Valri was a forever type of woman, the kind to take home to mother—if he had a mother to take her to. The kind who required settling down, drawing up blueprints for a tidy, two-story home that would house not just the two of them but two point five children and a mixed-breed dog, as well.

In short, everything he'd been running from all

his adult life, not because he didn't want it, but because he did. It would be wrong to get involved with that type of woman because he had nothing to give in return. Instability had been the main structure of his life, and a woman like Valri needed and deserved stability.

This was wrong, a little voice somewhere far in his soul was faintly shouting.

All wrong.

She had a pedigree, and he came from a family of con artists and art forgers. The two were hopelessly incompatible.

There were so many, so very many arguments for this not to be happening between them. And only one small argument for it taking place.

Because he wanted her.

Wanted her with every fiber of his being, and one taste of her did not satisfy that intense craving.

Instead, what it did was increase the desire to have her a thousandfold.

He threw away restraint, as well as common sense, and gave himself up to the hurricane of emotions swirling through him.

If nothing else, he wanted her to always remember this—because he would.

Each kiss flowered into the next, increasing her desire as well as her pulse rate. She was on fire and feeling out of control. That was a new sensation for her. She'd always been the one who calculated everything down to the smallest detail. But this time, with this man, that control had been yanked out of her hands.

Suddenly, she'd been swept up, dragged along, like a swimmer caught in a riptide. The only difference was that there was no fear attached, only pleasure, pleasure of the kind that took her breath away and had her inwardly begging for more.

Passionate kisses blazed the way for possessive caresses that became only more so.

He owned her from the first touch.

A sense of ever-heightening urgency caused clothing to be all but ripped away, leaving a trail that went from the door to his bedroom. Once they had crossed that threshold, wrapped up—and around— each other with absolutely nothing in the way except for the flames of desire, the urgency flared almost sky-high.

He wanted to make love with her right at that instant, to feel that delicious sensation of conquest, growing excitement and then release. But at the same time, he didn't want it to be over, didn't want this wonderful, dizzying foreplay to end.

Hearing the small gasps and cries of ecstasy from Valri's lips served to heighten his own ecstasy, his own pleasure.

If he could have planned his own eternity, his own version of heaven, it would have been this: to make love with this woman over and over again until the grains of sand ran out.

Alex had brought her up several times only to have her teetering on the brink, and then he'd retreat just enough to start all over again.

She was ready to explode, yearning for that final event, when everything lit up like the Fourth of July, showering stars all over her.

Her anticipation escalated.

Alex moved down her body, marking his path with quick, sensual hot kisses, causing her skin to dance and quiver of its own accord, further underscoring the fact that she had no control over her own body, her own reactions.

Her head swirling, she placed her hands on Alex's shoulders and stopped him before he could cause yet another tidal wave of sensations to come pouring out. Urgent tugs finally brought him back up to her level, his eyes on hers.

"Now," she whispered urgently. *"Now."*

The smile curving his mouth told her he understood. Weaving his fingers through hers, his eyes never leaving her face, Alex drew himself up and then into her, sealing their bodies together to form one whole being.

And then the dance began, the tempo at first slow, then a little faster, and a little faster than that. The pace increased, each one faster than the last, not as fast as the next.

Continuing in an upward spiral until there was no higher level left.

He was consumed with her, skillfully bringing them both up to the level they deserved. The one they had worked so hard to achieve.

When he felt it about to reach the pinnacle, Alex sealed his mouth to hers, a silent symbol of unity, proving he was as much hers as she was his.

The eruption enveloped them both and they clung to it for as long as they could, unwilling to descend to earth.

But the descent was inevitable.

When it was over and the euphoria was breaking up into tiny, tiny pieces and receding into the mist, he still cradled Valri in his arms, wishing for a better world than the one they were currently occupying.

And then, out of the blue, he laughed softly to himself. "I guess this wasn't exactly what you expected when I asked you to come in for a root beer."

A smile was flirting with her lips as she propped herself up on her elbow to look at him.

"Who says?" she challenged. "This is *exactly* what I thought was going to happen when I said yes and pretended to take you up on that offer."

"You didn't want root beer?"

"Not especially."

The warmth in his eyes had nothing to do with sex and everything to do with her. "Anyone ever tell you that you're devious?"

"You'd be the first," Valri answered innocently.

Sure he was, Alex thought, amused. "But I'll bet I won't be the last."

"I'll take that bet," she told him. "We'll talk terms later. Much later. Because I've got things for you to do at the moment."

If he planned to ask "What?" Alex never got the chance. She had better things to do with his mouth than just have him talk.

And she showed him.

Chapter 16

She brought out the best in him.

It was the first thought that whispered across his brain as Alex began to slowly surface above the layers of sleep that had been wrapped around him. While making love with a woman was a vastly pleasurable undertaking, in his experience, he rarely did an encore. Moreover, to the best of his recollection, making love three times in the space of one night had *never* happened before.

But then, Valri had happened and it seemed as if all the rules, all the givens suddenly changed.

Just thinking about last night aroused him. Eyes still closed, savoring the warm memories, Alex reached for her.

And came up with more blanket, but no Valri.

She wasn't there.

He bolted upright, fully awake now, and his eyes flew open. Her side of the bed was really empty.

When had she left? And, more important than that, why?

Alex was about to throw on his clothes in order to go search for her when he noticed that he wasn't the only one in the room. His brain still fuzzy, it took him a prolonged moment before he could actually focus.

He was staring at Valri's back.

She hadn't left, she'd just left his bed.

Valri was wearing one of his T-shirts. Now, why did that seem so incredibly sexy to him? But it did. Especially when he began thinking about the very real possibility that she had nothing on underneath the T-shirt.

She was seated at the small desk in the corner, and from what he could ascertain, Valri was typing something on his computer.

"You're up," she said without turning around.

Surprised, since he hadn't made any noise he was aware of, he began to ask, "How did you...?"

"I can see your reflection on the monitor," she told him, then added, "I made coffee."

That didn't interest him nearly half as much as what she was currently doing. "Are you on the computer?" he asked in disbelief.

He heard her laugh in response. "Looks like it, doesn't it?"

Obviously, for her it was business as usual. Was she that addicted to the internet? What was she checking? And, now that he came to think of it, how?

"But my computer is password protected," he protested.

Valri looked over her shoulder at him and grinned. The expression on her face told him that it would have taken more than just a simple password to lock her out.

"It was," she acknowledged. Her tone indicated that she was willing to leave it at that.

She might, but he wasn't. "You hacked into my computer?"

"Afraid so," she confessed. "I needed to follow up a hunch I just had and I left my own laptop at home. I thought I'd be finished before you woke up. Sorry," she apologized. But she didn't stop typing.

Alex leaned over the side of his bed and scooped up a pair of jeans that he'd forgotten about and left on the floor two nights ago.

Sliding the jeans on, he got up and walked up behind his partner. "You had a 'hunch' at—" he paused to look at his watch, the only thing he'd had on last night when he'd made love with her "—six thirty in the morning?"

Again she grinned. "My hunch had no idea what time it was," Valri quipped.

He found the whole idea slightly suspect. "What are you doing?" he asked. Just what had been so important it had her abandoning bed at this hour? "Updating your Facebook page?"

And then something else occurred to him, something that was closer to home, given the background she'd mentioned to him. "Don't tell me you're playing video games."

"No and no to both your questions," Valri answered. "I enjoy video games and I have to admit, there is a certain rush that comes when you're playing in competitions, but I can walk away anytime. I play the game, the game doesn't play me," she assured him. "I'm not addicted to video games—the way some people are."

"Are you talking about—?" He didn't get a chance to finish his question.

"Uh-huh. Bigelow," she confirmed. "He's evolved into a pretty savvy hacker, but deep down inside that hacker lives the soul of a gamer." Her fingers swept across the keyboard swiftly as she talked. "And, like any true addict, Bigelow can only stay away for so long before he picks up another controller and jumps into another competition."

He watched screen after screen go by at almost a dizzying speed. Was she searching for Bigelow this way, looking for the multiplayer game he had joined?

"Didn't you tell me that at any given hour, there were a lot of online tournaments going on at the same time?" he asked.

Valri remained focused on the screens that were whizzing by. "Yup, that was me. That's what I said," she agreed.

Fascinated by the speed with which she was typing, Alex dragged over the other chair he had in his bedroom. Some of the clothes that had resided on the back of it fell off as he parked it next to the desk. Straddling the chair, he continued to watch what she was doing. From where he sat, it seemed like a rather hopeless endeavor.

"Then isn't looking for Bigelow like this a little like looking for—"

"A needle in the haystack?" she supplied without looking away from the screen. "Yes, it is."

If it was an exercise in futility, he had a feeling she wouldn't have undertaken it, so he made no further comment.

Next to the computer he saw that Valri had parked one of his coffee mugs. The mug was empty. From the faint stain he saw inside, he knew it hadn't been that way for long.

"Want a refill on the coffee?" he offered.

She spared him a grateful glance. "That would be great."

Picking up the mug, Alex made his way into the kitchen. He smelled it a moment before he saw it. Valri had brewed an entire pot of coffee, most of which was still on the coffeemaker. After refilling her mug, he took one for himself.

Alex was carrying a mug in each hand as he walked back to the bedroom. He had almost made it back when he heard Valri declare a very enthusiastic and exceedingly pleased "Gotcha!"

Yes, you do, Alex thought in total and absolute wonder. She had him. *And I don't even know how you did it. All I know is that if I tried to fight this, it would easily qualify me to be number one on the list of dumbest human beings.*

"You know, bragging isn't very ladylike," he told Valri as he crossed the threshold into the room. He handed his partner her mug and then took a sip of his own jet-black coffee.

"Right now, I don't care," she answered in all honesty. "I feel like crowing, which isn't very ladylike, either," she acknowledged philosophically. Exceptionally pleased with herself, Valri leaned back in the faux leather swivel chair, holding the mug of steaming coffee with both hands. She stared at the screen, a very satisfied look on her face. "I got him, Alex. I got the SOB. He just couldn't keep away."

"Oh." He looked over her shoulder at the screen as the truth dawned on him for the first time. "You're talking about Bigelow."

"Well, yeah, of course I'm talking about Bigelow. Who did you think I was talking about?" The moment the question was out of her mouth, she realized the answer. Turning her chair so that she could face him, Valri smiled warmly. "I don't have to go on the internet in order to find you," she pointed out. "You're right here, bigger than life," she murmured just before she turned back to the computer monitor.

"So Bigelow is online right now?" he asked. He looked at the screen again, but he realized that it didn't matter how long he stared at it, he wouldn't see what she saw.

"That's where he is," she assured Alex.

"But that still doesn't tell us where he *physically* is. He's clever enough to have hidden his tracks," he pointed out.

Alex was standing behind her, one hand resting on her shoulder as he stared at some sort of a strange scenario, a medieval-looking world of intricate castles populated by perfect specimens of the ideal men and women engaged in battles using futuristic weapons.

"Wanna bet?" Valri paused what she was doing to look at him for a moment. "Do you even *know* what I do?" she asked.

His smile was extremely sexy as he pretended to think. "If memory serves, you have the power to up my stamina to levels I didn't know that I was capable of reaching."

Valri struggled not to laugh. "I meant on the computer."

That part he was already well aware of. "You make that damn thing talk to you the way it doesn't to most people—certainly not me."

"Close enough," she accepted. He was describing it as best he could, considering he was a layman. "What I just did, after following it to various places all over the world, was track down his IP address."

He'd heard the term a number of times and never really stopped to find out exactly what that meant or entailed. He asked now. "And that is...?"

"A good thing," she concluded, not wanting to confuse him with way too many details. "Bigelow is clever and took some heavy-duty precautions, bouncing his signal all over the place, but eventually it led to this address," she told Alex, typing said address on the keyboard so that it could be located on a map of the region.

"You see," she continued, "Bigelow thinks he's too smart to be caught and *that's* his tragic flaw, his hubris." When she caught the bemused look on her partner's face, Valri told him, "I minored in English lit. Some of it stuck."

"Anything you say," Alex replied, willing to accept whatever she told him. He affectionately kissed the top of her head. Then he got a pen off the desk and wrote down the address he saw on his palm since there was no paper around. "I'll call this in and request backup to meet us there."

"Let me see if anyone owns the building," she said, typing quickly again. In less than two minutes, she had gotten into public records to see if the property had been bought by anyone, or if it had just been completely abandoned, allowing transients and vermin to overrun the building.

"How do you *do* that?" he marveled, looking over her shoulder.

"Practice. Well, what do you know," she said under her breath.

"There is an owner?" Alex guessed.

"And it's none other than Jason Bigelow. Recent sale, too. He must have thought he needed a hideout," she told her partner.

He took out his cell phone again. "I'll be making that call for backup now."

"There's no real hurry," she told him, although she was experiencing a sense of urgency just because she wanted to catch and isolate the gamer who had fooled her. "It's a tournament, Brody. These things go on for very long periods of time. He's not going to be going anywhere for a while," she assured him. Getting up from the desk, she grasped his shoulders and paused long enough to deliver a long, deep kiss. "That's a retainer against later," she told him with a wink. "Now let's go catch us a hacker."

* * *

Jason Bigelow had taken up residence in what looked to be an old abandoned warehouse that had once been used to house the latest electronic equipment a couple of decades ago. A few could still be found tucked away on rusted shelves and covered with dust that had become part of the cardboard that surrounded each product, products such as Betamax recorders and other things that had fallen out of favor and then slipped away, unnoticed, out of society.

The company that stored its products in the warehouse had been forced into bankruptcy some eighteen years ago. Salvaging what it could, the defunct business left the warehouse to bear witness to its footprint. Bigelow had bought it for the proverbial song.

Using bull cutters, Alex cut through the old lock that barred access to the warehouse. It fell to the ground with a deep thud.

Setting the bull cutters aside, Alex asked, "You sure he's in here?"

"That's what the signal says. It's perfect," she told him. "The place was abandoned, Bigelow has it all to himself and there's probably wiring that he can put to his own use. This is his own slice of heaven, and best of all, his mother isn't living twenty yards away."

Weapons out and raised, adrenaline radiating

at what felt like peak level, Valri and Alex placed themselves at opposite sides of the warehouse doors. Alex pushed them ever so slightly. Without the lock holding them in place, the doors gave.

His eyes on Valri, he silently held up three fingers, mouthing a countdown. When Alex formed the word *one*, they went in, guns and flashlights crossed over one another.

At first glance, the warehouse appeared to be as empty as it was supposed to be. But a closer investigation allowed Alex to spot just a sliver of light evident in the space between the door at the far end of the warehouse and the doorsill.

"Just follow the light," Alex whispered to her as he led the way to the back.

Braced for anything, they crept from the warehouse doors to the door that was located all the way at the other end of the building.

The door that was undoubtedly meant to keep intruders out.

The closer they got, the clearer the sound that was emanating from behind the door became.

Looking in her direction. Alex cocked his head, as if to ask if that was the sound they were supposed to be hearing. He had absolutely no experience—and no desire to have experience—with video games.

Valri slowly nodded.

That was when Alex kicked the door in, shouting,

"Aurora Police Department! Show us your hands! Now! Jason Bigelow, you are under arrest for the murders of Hunter Rogers and Randolph Wills."

Rather than feigning innocence and attempting to talk his way out, now that that he had been exposed, Bigelow threw aside his controller and grabbed what appeared to Valri to be a gun that the gamer had kept right next to him as he played.

"You don't want to do that," Valri warned.

"The hell I don't!" Bigelow shouted back, discharging two quick rounds in her direction. He missed both times.

The bullets ricocheted, making a noise as they hit something metallic.

"Looks like you'd better stick to shooting people in the video games," Alex told him.

The instant Bigelow had gotten off the shots, Alex knocked him down. There was a short, intense struggle for possession of the handgun. Bigelow was very fast, but when it came to strength, Bigelow was the loser by a long shot.

All in all, the struggle was over almost before it had begun. Bigelow was in handcuffs within a matter of a couple of minutes.

Alex read the gamer his rights. Bigelow hardly seemed to hear them. Instead, he seemed to vacillate between timidity and outrage.

"It's a mistake! You're making a big mistake!"

he cried, frustrated as he yanked at handcuffs that were not about to give way.

"I think that big mistake belongs exclusively to you," Alex told him. "And if you don't stop whimpering like an overgrown baby, I'm going to gag you—or knock you out. Take your pick. Personally, I'd love an excuse to knock you out," he said. The sound of approaching squad cars pierced the air. "Sounds like your ride is here," he informed Bigelow.

"Whatever you want, your fondest dreams, I can make it happen," Bigelow said, talking fast as desperation set in. "Just let me go," he pleaded.

"Sorry, that train left the station a long time ago," Alex replied. "And as for my fondest dream, that would be to see you behind bars."

Less than two minutes later, the empty warehouse was filled with uniformed officers, weapons drawn and at the ready.

"All the excitement's over," Alex told the two policemen who were the first to arrive. "Take this piece of garbage down to the precinct and book him for double homicide. We'll be there to fill out the report in a few minutes," he promised.

"You got it, Detective," Owens, the officer closest to him, said obligingly.

Owens and his partner herded the gamer out. Predictably, Bigelow didn't go quietly. But Alex was no longer paying attention to the gamer. Something else was bothering him.

Valri's behavior was out of sync with her usual manner. She'd not only let him take the lead, but she had completely hung back, acting more like a shadow than a partner.

Something was off.

He turned toward her, about to ask her what was wrong, but before he could open his mouth, Valri beat him to the punch and asked her own question.

"Are you finished with Bigelow for the time being?" she asked, her voice oddly hollow.

"Well, since the officers just took him down to the precinct, I'd say that the answer is yes," Alex responded, thinking that was rather a strange question to ask.

"Good." Valri exhaled, then took in another shaky breath. That was when he noticed that she was perspiring in addition to looking rather pale. "Because I think I need a ride to the hospital," she told him.

Instantly alert, Alex drew closer, his eyes sweeping over her entire body, one side at a time. "Why?"

"Those bullets Bigelow fired? The ones that made that strange pinging sound? I think I know why the sound stopped," she told him. Running her tongue along her dried lips, she looked down at her left side. "One of them hit me."

And that was when he saw it. There was blood

slowly soaking into the pullover sweater that she had borrowed from him. The red stain was claiming more and more of the material even as they stood there. "I think I ruined your sweater," she told him weakly.

"The hell with the damn sweater," he bit off. Closing his arms around her, he forced her to the ground. "Stay down!" he ordered.

His cell phone was instantly in his hand and he hardly remembered pressing the number connecting him to the station. "I need a bus," he shouted into the phone, following up the terse statement with the one that always sent chills vibrating through officers and detectives alike. "Officer down. I repeat— officer down! Corner of Magnolia and Jamboree!"

Then he looked accusingly at the woman he'd forced to lie on the ground.

"Why didn't you tell me you were shot?" he demanded angrily, struggling to block out the possible consequences that could evolve from this scenario.

"I didn't realize that I was hit right away. And then I didn't want to interrupt you. You were doing so well," she told him, not realizing that she was whispering.

"Of all the crazy, stupid—"

He couldn't find the adequate words to finish his thought. That was when he heard it. A siren.

The ambulance was almost here.

He was afraid to be relieved, afraid not to.

"After they patch you up at the hospital," he said, deliberately treating her condition lightly because he couldn't handle the thought of it being otherwise, "I'm going to strangle you."

"It's a deal," Valri murmured just before she passed out.

Chapter 17

Full-figured with iron-gray hair she wore in a tight, slightly askew bun, Sophie Moorehead had been a nurse at Aurora Memorial since the day the hospital had opened its doors some forty-four years ago.

Throughout the years, she had survived the building's five makeovers, enduring remodeling dust and tripping over overzealous construction workers. She put up with it all with good grace and a sense of humor. But in the past few years, she found herself fondly longing for the days when visitors were restricted to only a few hours a day and even those were not all in succession.

"You people really should have your very own

hospital, or at the very least, your own annex to this one," she grumbled, trying yet again to get the concerned policemen and women to move out of the corridor into the room where friends and family were *supposed* to congregate. "It's called a waiting room for a reason, people," Sophie announced to the crowd in general. She looked around at them expectantly.

But none of the Cavanaughs seemed to hear what she had said, or if any of them heard, they pretended not to.

Her hands on her very ample hips, Sophie turned to look at Brian Cavanaugh, who had arrived in the third wave, looking more concerned than usual, which in her opinion was a great deal.

"Don't they ever follow the rules?" she demanded, looking at him accusingly, as if the overflow of police personnel was all his fault.

"Only when they absolutely have to," Brian answered. His customary genial, understanding smile was nowhere to be seen. Instead, his brow was furrowed and he looked as if the weight of the world was firmly on his shoulders. "Anything new?" he asked Sophie.

"From five minutes ago? No," she informed him tersely, treating him the way a seasoned teacher would handle a wayward student who needed to be set straight. "She's still in surgery. When I hear anything, you'll be the first to know."

Out of the corner of her eye, she saw three more
people coming down the corridor from the front
entrance. Scowling, she told them the same thing
she had told all the others who had come within the
past two hours. "Waiting room's right there." She
pointed to the space that was largely empty before
heading to the operating rooms.

Duncan Cavanaugh, accompanied by two of his
siblings, Brendan and Kelly, nodded absently at the
older woman in the blue scrubs. He'd seen the chief
of Ds and made straight for him.

However, Brendan was the first to reach the chief.
"Is it true?" he asked, trying not to worry but failing
miserably. Valri was the baby, the one they were all
supposed to protect. This kind of thing wasn't supposed to happen. "Was Valri wounded?"

Brian nodded grimly. He told them everything
that he knew so far. "The perp's bullet went wild,
ricocheted off something and hit her. She's still in
surgery. Her partner said she was lucid until a few
minutes before the paramedics arrived."

"What does that mean?" Kelly asked. "Is she getting worse?"

Brian shook his head. "Hopefully not" was all
he could honestly say.

Brendan looked closer at his superior and read
between the lines. "It's not your fault, sir," he said
quietly.

Brian hadn't said anything to anyone about that

so far, but the whole incident had been preying on his mind since he'd gotten the word. He was having a great deal of difficulty keep his guilt under wraps. Valri wouldn't have been shot if he hadn't put her on the case in the first place.

"Maybe I sent her in too soon. Maybe she could have used a little more on-the-job experience before I set her loose in the big leagues."

"Valri's Valri, sir. There's nothing that's going to change that. She was very proud that you picked her for this assignment," Kelly confided, speaking up. "She'll come through this. She's been a scrapper all her life. No reason to believe that this is different from anything else she's been through."

Brian looked over toward the closed doors that separated all of them from the operating rooms. "Still, maybe I didn't do your sister any favors by picking her for this."

"She didn't see it that way, sir," Duncan assured him.

The former chief of police approached and the trio took their cue and went to talk to some of the other detectives and patrol officers who were keeping vigil and bolstering each other's spirits.

"Here," Andrew said, placing a paper cup filled to the brim with steaming black liquid into his younger brother's hand. "You look like you could use this."

Brian blinked, looking down into the cup. The

overhead light shimmered across the black surface. "Coffee?"

"Looks like it," Andrew commented.

Brian took a sip, then looked at his older brother. "Irish coffee."

"I prefer to think of it as Scottish coffee. You looked like you needed something a little stronger than the sludge that comes out of these vending machines." He glanced at Brian's dubious expression. "Don't worry, I'll drive you home," Andrew promised.

In response, Brian took another sip. "How many times have we stood here like this, waiting to hear if one of our own made it or not?" he asked Andrew wearily.

"Too many times to count, although I'm sure that Nurse Smiley over there could probably give you the exact number," Andrew said, nodding over at the scowling head nurse. "Just for the record—to raise your spirits—we haven't lost a Cavanaugh yet."

"We did once," Brian reminded him grimly. Andrew looked at him. They were sharing the same thought. One of the first times they'd stood here, waiting with time dragging itself by, was when their brother had caught a bullet in the line of duty.

"You mean Mike?" Andrew said rhetorically. "I think that Mike chose to go that way. Taking a bullet was a lot easier than facing up to your mistakes if you're an emotional coward."

"And he was that, I guess," Brian agreed. That was never more evident than when their brother's secret family came to light. Married to one woman, he had still created a family with another.

True to her word, Sophie came out of the operating room and walked into the center of the waiting throng before she said a word.

"Detective Cavanaugh is out of surgery. It'll be a while before they take her from recovery to her room. At least an hour, if not more. Why don't you people pick someone to represent you and the rest of you can go home and stop blocking the halls?" Sophie suggested in a voice that would have made a drill sergeant proud.

The woman's small, sharp blue eyes swept over the crowd. No one was budging.

With a deep sigh, she shook her head and walked away, mumbling to herself. "Six more months to retirement, just six more months…"

For the past ninety minutes, Alex had stood like a sentry outside the operating room doors. When he saw the inner doors to Valri's operating room part, he instantly came to attention, watching every movement, searching for some sort of reassurance that everything had gone well.

He saw his partner being wheeled out toward another room he assumed was the recovery area. Alex continued to look through the small portal until there was nothing to see. The recovery room doors had swung closed, terminating his view of her.

"You know, I'm pretty sure that the wall'll stay up even without you propping it up with your back. Why don't you give it a try and sit down?" Sean Cavanaugh suggested. Though slightly shorter than his two brothers, his chiseled features, contrasted with his kindly smile, definitely identified him as a Cavanaugh.

Alex turned to look at the head of the day-shift crime scene investigation unit.

"Can't," Alex replied.

Sean looked at him with sympathy. "Knees forgot how to bend?"

"Something like that," Alex answered.

He didn't even bother trying to smile. He knew the older man was being kind and trying to raise his spirits, but right now it was all he could do to keep his imagination from running away with him.

If he'd just been a little faster, a little more observant and pushed her out of the way, Valri wouldn't be lying in recovery.

"My brother Andrew has some heartening statistics you might want to hear," Sean told the younger man. "We've spent a lot of man-hours in this hallway, waiting for news about one member of the police department or another. And in all that time, we've never lost a single person."

As far as Sean was concerned, there was no point

in talking about the brother he had never gotten to know. Alex didn't need to hear anything negative right now. There was more than enough going on in his immediate life right now.

"She's going to be all right," Sean said with conviction.

With his whole heart and soul, Alex wished he could really believe that.

"There are no guarantees, sir," Alex pointed out.

"No, there aren't," Sean agreed in an easy tone. "People don't come with warranties, which is why we have to make the very most of what we do have. Make every day count and seize happiness wherever you find it." He smiled then, thinking of the wedding they had all just attended. "Like my father, Shamus, just did."

Alex nodded. "You're right."

"I generally am." Sean patted him on the back, repeating what he'd said earlier. "She's going to be fine."

The first sensation Valri was aware of was pain. Dark, sharp, inescapable pain.

It had woken her up. Beginning as a distant pain, it grew more pronounced, as well as sharper, as sleep receded away from her on shaky legs.

Opening her eyes, Valri felt frighteningly disoriented.

She didn't recognize the bed, or the room, or the faint baby powder smell.

What *was* that?

It all translated itself into a single message: she didn't belong here.

Groggy, unable to focus, Valri still tried to throw off the covers and swing her legs out of bed.

For all the energy she *thought* she'd expended, all she really managed to do was move the covers a fraction of an inch away from her.

The second he saw her trying to move, Alex was on his feet. He stopped the blanket from going anywhere. He did the same with Valri.

"Hey, hold it, Cavanaugh," he cautioned her. "You can't get up."

The pain was close to cutting her in half. She couldn't seem to get away from it.

"Why not?" Valri challenged a beat before she passed out.

"That's why not," Alex murmured.

Looking down at her, he very carefully tucked the blanket back around her. Even anesthetized she was still feisty. For the first time since he'd accompanied her to the hospital in the ambulance, Alex began to relax a little.

She was going to be all right, he thought with a relieved smile. Sean and Andrew had been correct. They'd each said she was going to be fine, and she was.

Alex settled back in the chair and waited for her to open her eyes again.

"Oh God, I feel as stiff as a board," Valri groaned, trying desperately to locate a single part of her that didn't feel as if it had been run over by a moving van. She was conscious and this time she didn't drift in and out of disorientation.

She was fully awake.

She also instantly recognized Alex and felt self-conscious about looking, in her estimation, the worst she had in her whole life.

"How long was I out?" she asked him.

"Two," Alex replied after a beat. There was a lump in his throat the size of a golf ball. He was more relieved than he was ever going to possibly say.

"Two whole hours? No wonder I feel so stiff. This mattress feels like someone's trying to plant a rock garden."

"Not two hours," Alex corrected. "You were out for two days."

Valri looked at him in disbelief, absolutely stunned. "Two days?" she echoed incredulously. "Are you sure?"

He could recount every one of those two days in five-minute increments. "Yes, I'm sure. You were out that whole time."

"How would you know that?" she asked.

"Because I sat here that whole time," he told her, "waiting for you to wake up."

Her eyes grew huge. She wasn't sure if she believed him. Maybe he was just making it up. Who surrendered that much of himself?

"You sat here for two days?"

He nodded. "Your family would bring me food when they came to visit. Especially your uncle Andrew." There was just the slightest curve to his mouth. "That man can sure cook."

Valri cut him short, trying to get to the bottom of this story.

"They were here?" she asked Alex in awed wonder. "Who?" she pressed. When she got stronger, she wanted to thank them all personally. It seemed like the least she could do.

"Everyone," Alex told her with finality.

Valri was still having difficulty absorbing what this all meant. Or maybe she was having difficulty because there was no longer any control.

"By 'everyone' you mean—"

"I mean *everyone*. The head nurse in the ER area threatened to have everyone evicted, but since they were also the police, she had no one to call to do the honors. She wasn't happy about backing off. You would have gotten a kick out of it if you were conscious." He took her hand and looked at her with deep concern as well as mind-numbing relief. "How do you feel?"

She closed her eyes for a moment, searching for an adequate description that would do what she felt justice. "Like my body was taken to the science lab and rejected after they'd cut it up into tiny little pieces, so somebody pasted all those tiny pieces together."

Alex laughed drily. "Anyone rejecting you should have to have their head examined."

She smiled. That was sweet of him. It was also completely unexpected. "You're just saying that because I was shot—indirectly."

"I'm just 'saying' it because it's true," he contradicted. She was wriggling in the bed, as if she was searching for a comfortable spot and obviously couldn't find one. "You want me to call the nurse for you?"

"I thought you wanted me all to yourself," Valri teased, trying to rise above the pain or at least find a way to endure it until it finally faded.

"Not when you're in pain," he told her seriously. "Then I just want to get you help."

She gave him what she hoped was a brave smile. "It'll pass," she said, dismissing the subject. She was more interested in the one she raised next. "What happened with Bigelow?"

"Your collar is presently sitting behind bars, where he's going to be for a long while. Judge vetoed bail because with his skills, Bigelow can hack into the system, reverse the charges and book himself a flight to Switzerland, all at the same time."

He had lost her right from the beginning. "Wait. *My* collar?" She repeated the phrase he'd used. There had to be some mistake. "You were the one who tackled the guy and cuffed him."

"Which would never have happened if you hadn't tracked him down with your computer voodoo. So I figure the collar is yours. You deserve it. Besides," he reasoned, "things like that look good on your record when they're deciding whether or not to make you a permanent detective."

Her mouth dropped open. With a grin, Alex put his index finger beneath her chin and raised it, closing her mouth.

Valri stared at him, stunned. "You did that for me?"

The shrug was casual as well as dismissive. "Actually, I did that for me. Now that I've broken you in as my partner, I really don't feel like going through all that again with someone new." He spared another dismissive shrug. "I guess you're lucky I'm lazy."

"Yeah, lucky," she echoed with a wide smile. "Very lucky."

Granted, her whole body still had a postoperative ache to a great extent. But even so, she wanted to blow this Popsicle stand, the sooner the better. She had a feeling that right now, Alex was the best medicine for her. It certainly was worthwhile exploring.

"Can you get the doctor for me?" she asked him.

"Sure. I'll have the nurse page him." He crossed to the door and asked, "What should I say when she asks why you're asking for your doctor?"

"That I want him to discharge me so I can go home."

Hearing that, Alex turned around and walked back to her bed. "Not going to happen."

That surprised her. "Why?" she asked. "They patched me up, didn't they?"

"You were out of it for two days, Cavanaugh," Alex told her patiently. "They're going to want to watch you for a while—not that I can blame them."

"Brody—" There was a warning note in her voice. She wanted to go home.

"You're staying the night. Get used to it." He sat back down in the chair where he had kept vigil for the past fifty-one hours. "They've got a pretty good cable system here," he told her, picking up the remote control and aiming it at the flat-screen that was on the opposite wall. "They even get the Golden Movie Channel here. *Shane*'s playing." He hit the appropriate numbers to make the movie appear on the screen.

"Shane?" she questioned.

It was obvious that he was going to have to educate her. "It's a classic Western. The good guy wins and the bad guy gets his. You'll love it," he promised.

She knew when to accept the inevitable and right

now, in addition to acceptance, she knew she had a lot to be grateful for.

"If you say so," she said with a sigh.

Overwhelmed for a moment by what could have been a completely different outcome from the one they were experiencing, Alex leaned over the side railing of the hospital bed and kissed her.

"Welcome back, partner," he murmured. "Now, watch the movie."

"Yes, sir," she responded in an obedient, clipped tone.

"Music to my ears," he replied, referring to her humble demeanor just before he settled back beside her. Since the movie was already in progress, he treated her to a short narrative of what had happened in the story up to this point.

Valri hung on to every word, because he was saying them.

Epilogue

Alex fell back on her bed, spent and happily amazed. Amazed that the lovemaking between them just kept getting better and better rather than becoming routine or even old hat.

Every square inch of her bedroom was filled to the brim with the happiness she all but radiated from every party of her.

Valri had been forced to take the mandatory six weeks to recover from her wound and subsequent surgery and he had come over every night to be with her. Something, he had told her, he wanted to continue even after she went back to work the coming Monday.

Gathering her into his arms, he looked for a way to initiate the conversation he had been holding off having all during her convalescence.

"You know," Valri told him as she curled into his arms, "you don't have to treat me as if I was going to break any second."

He supposed that he had been extra careful around her. But who could blame him?

"You almost did," he reminded her. "And it was on my watch."

She smiled and shook her head. "Even if you were telepathic—which, by the way, I'm glad you're not—you wouldn't have been able to foresee that one of the bullets was going to ricochet and hit me. Odds were pretty much against it," she told him. "Lighten up, partner. I've been cleared for work. I get to come back next Monday."

He knew she was cleared—she'd told him enough times—but he was still worried. "You don't think that's rushing it a little?"

She looked at him as if he'd suddenly begun talking in a foreign language.

"Rushing it? Are you kidding? I'm going stir-crazy—not that I don't enjoy you coming over every night and reminding me that there's more to life than just work—but I *really* do need to get back to doing something useful before I lose my mind."

Cradling her in his arms, he kissed the top of her

head. "And burning up the sheets every night doesn't strike you as useful, huh?" he asked, amused.

"Very thrilling," she admitted, because she loved the idea of listening for his knock on the door, "but not exactly useful, no."

"I see," he murmured, this time pressing a kiss to the side of her neck.

She sighed, ready to slip back into the delicious world that they always created whenever they got together like this. "Did you really sit by my bed for two days like you said?"

The question had come out of nowhere and it took him a moment to focus. "Two days, three hours and twelve minutes to be exact."

She laughed and shook her head. How could someone become so dear to her so quickly? But there was no use fighting it. He had and what he just said sealed that position for him. "I had no idea you were so detail oriented."

"One of my many hidden talents," he told her.

He wanted to make love with her again, but he couldn't put this off any longer. To keep pushing it aside for one reason or another was to blatantly avoid the issue—and also to go on like this with her for another day. But while it was wonderful, making love with her like this, he caught himself wanting more.

Something permanent.

It was as big a surprise to him as it would probably be to Valri, he thought. But he had to take the next step. He *needed* to take it.

"As I sat there in your room, I had a lot of time to think."

Lying beside him, Valri languidly traced swirls along his chest. "Oh, about what?"

He wondered if she had a clue that she was really arousing him with those gliding fingertips of hers. He caught her hand in his, closing his fingers around it. Now that they were talking, he needed to get this out, and what she was doing was really interfering with his ability to think coherently.

"About what it would be like if you never opened your eyes again."

"Now there's a less than happy thought," Valri commented.

"Exactly," he agreed wholeheartedly. His tone grew very serious as he continued. "It made me realize that even though we've only been together a short time, I've gotten very used to seeing you."

"Is this where you break into a Rex Harrison imitation and sing that you've grown accustomed to my face?" she asked, trying to keep a straight face.

"Maybe later—and only if I want to torture you," he said. "I never thought that marriage, kids, all that average domestic business, was for me. I don't exactly have a normal family life in my background."

"Who does?" she asked with a dismissive shrug.

"You, for one. Your people believe in protecting

and serving." He paused for just a moment, knowing there was no turning back once this was out. "Mine believe in helping themselves."

Sounded like good old Yankee ingenuity to her. "Hey, there's nothing wrong with that."

He wasn't finished. "To other people's things."

"What?" Valri looked at him, confused. She was certain she hadn't heard him correctly.

He took a breath, then told her. "My family is made up of con artists, art forgers and grifters."

Was he trying to be funny? "You're kidding, right?"

But Alex shook his head. "I only wish I was."

"But you're a police detective," she stressed, confused.

"And for that I'm considered to be the black sheep of the family," he replied. That was all he could bear to say right now, and even that was difficult enough. He searched her face, wondering if he'd lost her for good. "I've never told anyone else about my family."

"But on your initial application to the police academy—"

"Parents deceased." He parroted the words he'd written in. "No siblings."

He would have been dismissed immediately if the fact that he'd lied on his application ever came to light, she thought. Right or wrong, Valri made up her mind at that moment that it would never come from her. "And you're telling me why?"

"Because I trust you and because I think you should know everything in my past before I ask you."

Their eyes met for a timeless moment as silence enveloped the bedroom. And then, smiling, Valri said, "Yes."

"Yes?" he echoed uncertainly. "But you don't even know what I'm going to ask you."

She gave him a knowing look. "I have an above-average IQ and I'm fairly certain that you're going to ask me to marry you. If you're not," she allowed gamely, "this is going to turn into a very embarrassing moment for both of us."

"Well, then I wouldn't dream of embarrassing you," he whispered against her cheek.

She drew her head back just a little so she could look at him. "That's very considerate of you."

"See, I told you. I just get better as time goes on," he told her. And then his grin softened into a smile. "I love you, you know."

Her eyes were shining as she said, "To be honest, I suspected as much, but I wasn't sure."

"Now you are," he said with finality. He waited a moment, but she remained as quiet as he was. "Isn't there something you want to say to me?"

She pretended to think for a moment, then said in all innocence, "I already said 'yes,' so no, can't think of anything offhand."

"You're going to drive me crazy like this for the next forty years, aren't you?" Alex guessed.

Her grin all but encompassed her entire face. "Count on it. And if you think you're getting time off for good behavior, say after forty years, think again. I'm going for the *long* haul, mister." She brushed her lips against his, then pulled back, teasing him. "And just for the record, yes, I love you, too. But that's one of those things that just go without saying."

"Not for me. I need to hear it," he told her.

"I'll keep that in mind," Valri promised. She was all but glowing as she said, "You do realize this means another Cavanaugh-style wedding, don't you?"

"I never thought I'd hear myself say this, but I can't wait," Alex told her.

There was just the right amount of enthusiasm in his voice. She knew he was telling the truth.

"Neither can I," Valri whispered as she wrapped her arms around his neck.

The time for talking was over.

* * * * *

"You're going to drive me crazy like this for the next forty years, aren't you?" Alex guessed.

Her grin all but encompassed her entire face. "Count on it. And if you think you're getting time off for good behavior, say after forty years, think again. I'm going for the *long* haul, mister." She brushed her lips against his, then pulled back, teasing him. "And just for the record, yes, I love you, too. But that's one of those things that just go without saying."

"Not for me. I need to hear it," he told her.

"I'll keep that in mind," Valri promised. She was all but glowing as she said, "You do realize this means another Cavanaugh-style wedding, don't you?"

"I never thought I'd hear myself say this, but I can't wait," Alex told her.

There was just the right amount of enthusiasm in his voice. She knew he was telling the truth.

"Neither can I," Valri whispered as she wrapped her arms around his neck.

The time for talking was over.

* * * * *

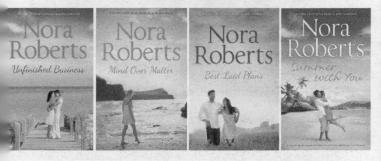
15_ST_11

MILLS & BOON®
INTRIGUE
Romantic Suspense

A SEDUCTIVE COMBINATION OF DANGER AND DESIRE

A sneak peek at next month's titles...

In stores from 17th April 2015:

- **Scene of the Crime: Killer Cove** – Carla Cassidy
  and **Navy SEAL Justice** – Elle James

- **Cowboy Incognito** – Alice Sharpe
  and **Under Suspicion** – Mallory Kane

- **Showdown at Shadow Junction** – Joanna Wayne
  and **Two Souls Hollow** – Paula Graves

Romantic Suspense

- **Capturing the Huntsman** – C.J. Miller
- **Protecting His Brother's Bride** – Jan Schliesman

Join our *EXCLUSIVE* eBook club

FROM JUST £1.99 A MONTH!

Never miss a book again with our hassle-free eBook subscription.

★ Pick how many titles you want from each series with our flexible subscription

★ Your titles are delivered to your device on the first of every month

★ Zero risk, zero obligation!

There really is nothing standing in the way of you and your favourite books!

Start your eBook subscription today at www.millsandboon.co.uk/subscribe